Contents

This story is for all the quiet weird kids: the ones who interacted with other kids only out of necessity, that would rather spend their time exploring the vast universe of imagination in their mind than socialize with any human. The ones who were made fun of for social ineptitude or unusual speech patterns, but knew how to interact with the characters in the worlds of their making. The ones who were pestered by their parents, insisting that playing outside would be more beneficial than reading or playing video games. I was one of those kids, and I'm proudly probably going to be one of those *women* for the rest of my life.

For everyone back in the Wattpad days when I first shared this story, and supported me even when I did weird things like making my characters be besties with Final Fantasy characters, your support back then means more than you could ever know. I hope this published version makes you proud to have placed your support in me.

Prologue

I n the beginning, there seemed to be nothing there; nothing in that expanse of space and the stars.

There were the planets in the distance. Earth and its moon, of course. And oh, the stars; more than trillions of stars, each sparkling brightly in the deep sky. But in that expanse— that space within the distance of light-years of Earth- apart from the moon, there was nothing that could be seen.

Nothing that could be seen by the unfiltered human eye, at least.

In the beginning, within that expanse— when, once again, there seemed to be nothing— there lived six goddesses, inhabiting a pocket of space that was parallel to Earth, each of them representing a particular element: wind, earth, fire, water, light, and darkness. They all usually got along quite well... so well that, after so long, they got bored; as one tends to do when there is no conflict to be had.

With nothing else to do, these goddesses decided to begin a project to occupy their time, as well as test the extent of their abilities.

After days of trial and error, the first result of their experimentation was a new, albeit much smaller, mass of land sitting parallel to Earth. But a giant mass of land by itself was hardly exciting or useful— this they all agreed. So, the goddesses decided to test themselves further, and after some time were able to create an entire ecosystem. Weather, air, sediment... all features usually found on Earth, replicated successfully on this smaller mass.

This mass would come to be known colloquially as the "magical world," for its lands and waters were made completely of magical substance. Its lakes, rivers, plains, and mountains were all formed by a concentration of magic so compact that it materialized into firm forms of matter, and the life that sprang forth was too made of magic.

But in time, this also wouldn't do. An ecosystem that ran smoothly invited no conflict, no excitement. If nothing else was done, then in time, things would become just as boring as they had been before.

The goddesses had to convene and ponder the situation for a long while. They needed to solve their boredom problem, and they needed to do it in a way that would be everlasting, not something that could easily be remedied— because then they'd go back to being bored again. Their solution could be considered extreme, but was the only one they could think of that would persist forever.

This world needed residents. Human residents.

Humans would reproduce. Humans would affect the ecosystem in varying ways; they'd have disputes with each other, explore, craft, create art; inspire one another. They would constantly bring new situations and new dilemmas to the magic world for millennia to come. With humans' instinctive discord, it was almost a certainty that the goddesses would never be bored again.

At first, the goddesses attempted to create their own humans, but the resulting life forms were lumpy and misshapen; incapable of speech or fine motor skills. These life forms also lacked the varying personalities that humans possess, so they weren't capable of activity apart from walking and falling over. With this idea not working, they then devised a plan: to populate their new magic world, they'd gather existing humans from Earth. They'd blur these humans' memories of Earth, so that they would still be able to speak, move, and retain their personalities and familial bonds, and conceal the two worlds from each other: in an attempt to both keep the two worlds separate, and keep the humans from remembering and longing for their past lives.

In time, the humans that were placed on the magic world began to absorb the magic of the land, and became magical beings themselves, in a way. They were able to use small amounts of magic, from spontaneously generating flames and icicles to cultivating plants. The goddesses encouraged this; but, recognizing how dangerous it could be if left unchecked, their mitigation was to limit each person's abilities to one school of magic.

At first, things were peaceful. The goddesses looked on, always interested in the happenings of the magic world. Watching it became like watching their children grow, as if the six were proud parents of humanity in this world. (And in a way, they were.)

That was all a long time ago.

There was one day with no moon where a congregation of dark clouds enveloped a small corner of the magic world. Such a small corner that, by the time the goddesses had noticed it, it was already too late to take action against it. Misfortune had sunk its fangs into the soil of the world, and now misery loomed in the air over that area of the world.

The malediction of this specific region was so strong that the goddesses feared intervening, lest it sap all of their power. They almost decided to let it be. However, noticing that the radius of misfortune completely enveloped the origin point of magic— the very foundation of this world, what kept it living and floating— they knew they had to do something to save it, as soon as the time was right; or else, the entire world would die.

And so the story begins...

Chapter One

Of No Consequence

On one particularly unremarkable autumn morning in a normally quiet suburb, a clock radio switched on, the sound of pop-punk marking 6:30 a.m. and filling the interior of the room, with its midnight blue walls and black cherry furnishings. The owner of the room, a red-haired high-schooler, woke up in a tizzy; unsure if this was reality, or if she was still dreaming; she pushed her curly hair into a bun in one swift motion as she attempted to recover her wits.

Sitting up, she recognized her room; its walls containing the occasional band poster, or framed reproductions of notable historical sites and occurrences. On the other side of the room, on the desk where she'd do her homework, sat a pink salt lamp and a stack of books, usually used for her classes. One of them lay open, most likely her French workbook. When she rose from her bed, pushing the fluffy hot pink duvet aside, she could feel the fuzzy tan carpet underneath her feet. There was no doubt about it: this was home.

With that out of the way, she walked over to her unkempt closet with its sliding white shuttered doors already opened, prepared to get ready for the day.

"That was such a strange dream. It felt so real that I almost couldn't tell the difference between when I was asleep and when I'd woken up. 'Course, I'm clearly awake now. Awake and in my room, and needing to get dressed for school..." she sighed.

Jaiden Winchester was currently in her first year of high school, and while she didn't exactly take her school duties seriously, she also didn't want to be seen as a slacker, so it was important that she didn't get to school too incredibly late... even if she did occasionally ditch classes. Today, though, she'd been able to wake up with her first alarm for the day— so the chances of her being late today were, thankfully, slim. After deciding on a plain khaki sweater-dress with forest green leggings underneath, she set out for the lower level of her house, quickly descending the flight of carpeted stairs to reach the kitchen.

Usually, this was where her parents would be sitting. Today— either due to her unusual earliness, or her parents going into work early, perhaps both— there was no one. Jaiden had siblings, but they no longer lived here. They were all adults now, and all but one lived in different parts of the country; so, if her parents weren't around, that meant she was alone for the time being. Deciding that this meant there was no good reason to stick around, Jaiden put on the first pair of shoes she recognized as her own and left, on her way to school. The brown knee-high boots she picked up weren't made to be warm, but they were still of adequate comfort and warmth for a chilly October day in the midwestern United States.

"That dream..." Jaiden said to herself as she walked leisurely to school, passing the row of bungalows on the end of her block. She made sure to look out for cars before walking into this intersection, knowing that this particular one had a problem with drivers refusing to slow down, even with a school nearby.

"There wasn't really anything out of the ordinary, was there? Maybe that's why it felt so realistic. Slice of life and all that, but I can't quite put my finger on it... something just felt *off* about it. It's like how something just feels so unnaturally serene that it's practically screaming, 'hey, we're hiding something underneath the—'"

"Ow! Hey!"

"Oh. Sorry." Jaiden apologized to the fellow student that she had accidentally run into. She didn't recognize them. They didn't look too pleased, but at the very least, they didn't continue to hassle her about it.

With that, Jaiden had reached her school: it could best be described as an old, almost historic building trying desperately to adapt itself into the new millennium. The remnants of its concrete brick-laden and stained glass past remained in its white peaks, reminiscent of old Roman Catholic churches, but so too were they lined with chrome beams of... steel, if Jaiden had to guess (likely to reinforce the pillars) and there was even a specific part of one of the roofs where solar panels had been installed. The short walkway leading toward the school's entrance was lined with trees that flowered in the spring, as well as multiple other plants. But since it was now autumn, the leaves on the trees had shifted into riveting orange and red hues, and most of the other plants had begun to shrivel up in the way they did when the weather got colder.

It was still early, so Jaiden wasn't sure where to go now that she was at school. Fortunately, she didn't need to think about it too long though, because she then noticed her favorite person was now being dropped off in front of the school.

Mishaela Pagliardi had been Jaiden's best friend since they were in the fifth grade, and at this point, they were virtually inseparable. Mishaela was slightly shorter than Jaiden, and had long wavy, thick hair that was pitch-black, with pale yellow highlights she'd had added at the beginning of this school year. She wore purple-rimmed square glasses over her warm-toned hazel-green eyes, and was the chubbier one of the duo, if only slightly— but she was clearly the more busty one of the two. Her fair skin had olive undertones, hinting toward her Mediterranean ancestry, and today she was wearing a simple red plaid A-line dress with a white blouse underneath, a simple floral pattern embroidered onto its Peter Pan collar.

Today, Mishaela was being dropped off with her older sister Chiara, who was two years her senior. Jaiden always made sure to say "older sister" and not "big sister," because Chiara was noticeably smaller than Mishaela in both height and weight, and had been for a long time now. She had the same hazel-green eyes as her sister, and her long hair was colored a bright shade of aqua. She was wearing a simple pair of black distressed jeans and a purple t-shirt with some type of vaporwave graphic on it, all pulled together with a black denim vest. Jaiden remembered this vest back when it had been plain, but it had since been adorned with plenty of silver studs and a couple of patches that were too small to be read from this distance. Unlike her sister, Chiara didn't wear glasses, and her skin was considerably more fair— pale, even.

"If it isn't my favorite pair of sisters!" Jaiden waved. "Hey, Mishaela, Chiara. Lovely brisk day we're having here, isn't it."

"Jaiden! Oh, my, you're here early. What's the occasion?" asked Mishaela. "Is everything all right?"

"What do you mean, 'is everything all right?'" Can't I just show up to school early for the first time in... uh, actually, I think this might be the first time since we started high school that I've gotten here early. You may have a point. Anyway, to answer your question: I had a weird dream, and couldn't sleep. Because of it, I woke up so early that my parents weren't even up yet, so I just came here since I needed the walk to think to myself. Hey, can I borrow you to talk about it? You're the brains in this outfit."

"That's fine with me. As long as Chiara is okay with it?" replied Mishaela, the end of her sentence rising in inflection as she turned to her sister.

"Hm? O-oh!" Chiara quickly turned to the two youths, trying her best to hide the fact that she hadn't really been listening. "Yes, that's fine. If Jaiden is at school this early, this is probably that important to them."

Jaiden smiled upon hearing her response. Over the summer, she'd asked the people close to her to try out referring to her with different pronouns so she could see how she felt about it— and these days, Chiara was the best at remembering to do so. "Thanks, Chiara. See you after school." Jaiden waved.

"Mm." Chiara nodded. "Have a good day."

"So, what dilemma have you found yourself in now?" asked Mishaela, as the two began to walk. "You mentioned having some sort of weird dream."

"Yeah. And it wasn't weird as in, like having the ability to fly and seeing horses with a cow's head weird. I guess it was pretty normal, in comparison. It was like I was in this small village, walking around with some cloak on and talking to this group of people. My memory's too blurry to remember their faces, but based on their voices, I don't think they were people I know in real life, or at least not people who are close to me. Anyway, I was walking along with them. We get to this fountain in some plaza, and one of the people-shaped blobs mentions being unable to get beef, and shaking their fist at this huge red building that was also blurry. Hm. You know, Mishaela— before, this dream felt unnervingly normal to me, but now that part's sticking out to me, not being able to buy beef. That's such a specific detail for my brain to include."

"It is," agreed Mishaela. "What's more: I know there are certain countries or regions where the people don't eat beef for religious or cultural reasons, but the way you phrase it makes it sound more like the people in your dream meant that it was available at a point in the past, but no longer was. A beef shortage, perhaps..?"

That's it. You have to familiarize yourself with these circumstances...

A voice foreign to Jaiden's mind echoed through her brain while Mishaela continued to talk.

The circumstances of a people who have suffered for far too long.

Being a racial minority, Jaiden was familiar with the concept, for sure.

Do you value your freedom? Is it something you wish for everyone to have?

Well, sure. That was why Jaiden was the way she was: all in the name of personal freedom. There were, of course, freedoms that she didn't necessarily have both as a Black girl, as feminine-presenting, and as a teenager. But even so, she was aware that there were people less fortunate than she in the freedom department; and if she had the power, she'd make it so that they'd be as free as they so desired.

It's admirable. But of course, you know that there is always an obstacle in the path to liberation.

This is what you must eradicate.

"...in a few days. Jaiden, are you listening to me?"

Know that this is not a dream, or your imagination.

"Jaiden?"

"Uh... yeah... absolutely. Of course I'm listening. Why don't we hit up the cafeteria for breakfast? Or at least to see what they're offering today," replied Jaiden, feeling ever-so-slightly dizzy. Maybe getting some food into her system would start to make things make sense... and even if it didn't, she was starting to get hungry, anyway. "Maybe since we're here so early, the food will taste better since it'll be fresh. Plus, I get to tell you all about this cute transfer student in my art class."

Mishaela sighed. "Another one?"

"I don't mean it in an attraction way, she's a girl! I mean, she *is* really cute, but that's why I want to be her friend; I like her style. I think you guys would get along too, based on your overall... girly aesthetic. And hey, maybe if you get along well enough, the two of *you* could pursue something a little more romantic than—"

"Goodbye, Jaiden," Mishaela said firmly, in the way she always did when she wanted the conversation to end; leaving Jaiden to hurry after her on the way to the cafeteria.

Chapter Two

She Came In A Dream

The next day, Jaiden woke up with an intense start; she couldn't remember the details of her dream anymore now that she was awake, but the feelings of urgency and dread remained.

She struggled to get her footing and fell onto the carpet underneath her bed, and took a moment to get reoriented before her gaze fell on the clock.

7:30 a.m. Frazzled *and* running late. What a combination.

This meant that there wouldn't be much time to do... well, anything, especially since she needed to shower before heading out. She rushed through the shower and brushed her teeth, grabbing the first few articles of clothing that looked and smelled presentable (a purple long-sleeved shirt, and a plain pair of blue jeans) at a glance, and once she was dressed, she sped downstairs. Her hair was still slightly damp, but she also knew it would dry on the impending run to school, so it didn't worry her too much.

Jaiden quickly glanced at the breakfast her mother had out on the table and grabbed a pancake and a piece of ham, taking one of each and rolling it up like a little jelly roll, eating it so quickly that she narrowly missed biting her tongue.

"Where's the fire?" her father joked then.

Initially, she hadn't even noticed he had been there, let alone that he had been joking. "Huh?" she asked, a piece of food falling out of her mouth and onto the table. She would usually try to catch it, but it was the least of her worries right now.

"I put a lot of work into my breakfast every day, Jaiden," her mother said. "The least you could do is chew it. Pick that up, don't be nasty."

Jaiden pushed her (negative) thoughts about her mother's cooking aside; there were bigger issues at hand. "There's no time!" she said frantically, despite those thoughts- but she did make sure to pick up the food she'd dropped. "Someone needs me, and I don't know where to find them, or why they need me... I need answers!" She stamped her foot in frustration at the end of her sentence, punctuating just how badly she needed those answers.

Her parents' response was to laugh, in the way that parents laughed when their children did something that tickled them.

"What's so funny?" Jaiden provoked them. She didn't find this as funny, clearly.

"It was just a dream, girl," her mother said. "Now, come on. Eat your food. I have to take your father to the airport, so you have plenty of time before I shuttle you off to school. And stop talking with your mouth full; it's disgusting."

Jaiden sighed. "In case you've been too self-absorbed as usual to notice, I am late. School starts in like... fifteen minutes. I don't need your ride," she said cruelly. Before either of them could demand for her to come back so they could scold her for being rude, she was running to school. Their house was only three blocks away, anyway, so a ride wasn't necessary. At the moment, though, the reason she was in a rush was because she just wanted to get to her school's library, convinced that there would be something there to help her decipher her dream— the thing that had her in such a frenzy today. She wasn't sure why she believed this, but then again, Mishaela always did say that the best way to learn about unfamiliar subjects was to consult the written word, and the library at school was the biggest, most close-by, and easily accessible place to do just that.

While she was running, Jaiden noticed that the shirt she was wearing had a mustard stain on the left sleeve, possibly from when corn dogs were being served at school. That had been last week, hadn't it?

Her jeans were fine, but she saw— as the legs flared up with every step as she ran— that her socks didn't match. Her shoes were also beginning to pinch her feet, because they were slightly too small; they had been borrowed from a friend.

I'm a hot mess. Oh, well, I can't go back now; I was already late, I'm already more than halfway there, and it's too risky. I do not have the time for a lecture today.

She entered the main building with a quick greeting to the school guards, and walked hastily toward the library, which was large enough in scale to have its own building, attached to the rest of the school via a couple of short hallways. There were two levels of books, the second level being made accessible by a flight of ornate stairs, with a small iron-wrought gate at their halfway point, which was usually closed during the before-school hours. The most striking aspect of the building was undoubtedly its roof, a mesmerizing dome of stained glass that cast gorgeous rainbows upon the main floor at noon if there was enough sun that day.

A very strong *ugh* permeated Jaiden's thoughts.

"I hate coming to this place, but I guess it's a necessary evil if I want any peace of mind about this dream..." she said to herself. "Alrighty then. I gotta pull myself together. We can do this, Jaiden."

As she looked around more carefully, Jaiden realized she wouldn't know where anything was, because of how rarely she came here. She could ask the librarian, but that would open the door to a bunch of tedious small-talk questions that she lacked the patience to handle right now. But all was not lost, for she knew just who to ask when it came to library issues— and she spotted her at one of the tables with a stack of books, reading one.

"Mishaela!" she yelled, and then realizing she was in a library, she whispered an apology to the librarian (since she was the only other person there at the moment).

Jaiden took a seat next to Mishaela, who was wearing her favorite sweater-dress today. It was pink with a black silk fluffy skirt, and had a turtleneck-like collar with small black buttons in the front. Jaiden thought— and said, often— it looked like something a seven-year-old should be wearing, but Mishaela absolutely adored it.

"I had the weirdest dream last night, and like, I thought I forgot it but now I remember it again. There was this, there was a lady... she searched for me, and wanted me to help her... she knew my name and everything..."

Although she was having a hard time articulating it, this is what Jaiden's dream had been:

She had been walking home from school when an unfamiliar woman interrupted her path. This woman wore a majestic red silk sari with silver embroidery, and had smooth skin the shade of brown that evoked imagery of sunsets on the shoreline sand. There had been a moment of unnerving silence, but when the woman finally spoke, she explained that she'd been looking for her for a long time. Jaiden had insisted she had the wrong person, and in response, the woman proceeded to tell her things she knew about her to confirm she wasn't mistaken: her name, her parents' and siblings' names, the school she went to, things she disliked, her allergies, and so on. The woman had then held out her hand and asked Jaiden to join her, and at that point, Jaiden had run away. It had creeped her out way too much.

However, judging by the look on Mishaela's face, Jaiden knew she'd done a horrible job of getting all of that out.

"You think I'm crazy." Jaiden sighed. "So did my parents. They were all like, 'It's just a dream,' and they just dismissed it. They just... it was like they didn't care. You know how my parents are. But this was way too surreal to be just a dream. You know how you have a dream, and you just, you just *know*? Well, this is one of those dreams. I know it means something." She was so frustrated that her eyes were teary, which was rare for her. "I have to—"

"I believe you," Mishaela's voice echoed through the area.

Jaiden gasped, and hastily pulled Mishaela into a hug, which took her by surprise. "Thank you," she said. "Thank you so much. I really needed that."

As someone opened the door to the library, the incoming wind blew Mishaela's hair, and she smiled. "You're welcome," she said, in that calm tone of hers. "I believe you because I had the same dream."

Jaiden gasped again. She and Mishaela had a lot in common, but they'd never had the same dream before, even after all these years. "You did?" she asked. "You mean, you were leaving school, en route to your house when you got interrupted by some weird lady that somehow knows very specific details about you?"

"No, I wasn't going to my house." Mishaela shook her head, straightening her glasses. "I was going to *your* house."

Jaiden listened as Mishaela described the dream she had had the previous night. Except for the part where the woman knew everything about Jaiden- predictably, it was adapted to Mishaela- detail for detail, their dreams had been exactly the same.

"It's a strange phenomenon, certainly. I wonder what it all means," Mishaela said then.

"Well, I can tell you one thing," Jaiden said to her. "I might have thought so before, but now I'm convinced we aren't gonna find out by sitting around here."

She stood up, dramatically.

"My dad is leaving for Boston, and my mom should be on her way to work by now if she's already dropped him off at the airport, so my house should be free. Come on, let's go."

When Jaiden began to walk, Mishaela grabbed her arm, stopping her. "Now, when you say that, do you mean 'go' as in leaving the library, or 'go' as in— are you seriously talking about—" she lowered her voice to a whisper– "school-ditching?! We can't do that, Jaiden. Imagine: all the work we'll get behind on, what this'll do to our permanent records and reputations as students. We can forget about good references for university." She gasped. "They'll call our parents! This is a bad idea. Bad, bad, bad."

Sigh. Mishaela's honor-student tendencies are really dragging me down.

"All right. Got it. Should've seen this coming," Jaiden replied. "Look at it this way: my two options are going, or going with you. Do you really want me to go out into the world, unsupervised, without your watchful eye presiding over me?"

"That certainly didn't stop you before now," Mishaela pointed out.

"Yeah. You're right. " Jaiden nodded. "It didn't. But this is different from me leaving because I wanted pizza or something. This is a matter of... possibly supernatural and otherworldly nature. You cannot stand there and tell me you're completely, a hundred percent okay with leaving something like that up to just me to solve."

Mishaela closed her eyes and exhaled a bit, which indicated to Jaiden that she was beginning to win her over. "It's not that I'm not at all curious. You know that I am. It's just that... I don't think you realize how much you're asking me to consider. How do I choose between the abyss of possible supernatural mystery, and my very real and certain future?"

Jaiden put her hands on Mishaela's shoulders. "Mishaela, first of all, we're freshmen," she said. "No one's gonna even remember the stupid little things we do now when it's time for a university. 'Specially not you, since we both know you won't be making this a habit. Now, chill. I got this."

"Do you really, Jaiden? Do you really got this?"

"I do! And if, for some reason, we end up getting caught or otherwise in some kind of trouble for anything stemming from this situation, I will take all of the blame. All of it. You were just my completely unwilling but ultimately powerless accomplice, all right? I'll even coach you on how to look extra helpless. Crying helps."

"Well..." Mishaela started. "I guess I couldn't ask any more from you than that. But I reserve the right to disappear from this scheme if I think it's starting to get too sketchy or dangerous."

"Absolutely. I'll even smuggle you back into the school, completely undetected. Now, let's be off while the crowds in the hallway give us a good cover." Jaiden took her by the hand, but was stopped by Mishaela's uncertain and slow pace.

"Off where, exactly?" she asked.

"Oh yeah, right." Jaiden had to remember that, even though the route was second nature to herself and her other friends, it wouldn't be so obvious to people like Mishaela. "The small door west of their school's gym."

Amidst many more small complaints and copious panicking from Mishaela, they both eventually made it out of the building safely, hopefully not being detected by any faculty or cameras. They walked for a few blocks before arriving at a fast food restaurant located about a block or two away from school, and after getting situated in a booth, Jaiden dialed the number for their school on her phone, selecting the extension for the attendance office.

It's times like these where I'm glad I sound exactly like my mother on the phone, Jaiden thought to herself. *I can get her mannerisms down, right? Yeah. I absolutely can. I live with her, so I should know how she acts by now.*

"You hungry?" she asked Mishaela as they both waited for the office to pick up.

"How could I possibly be hungry, with the amount of stress you're putting me through right now?" asked Mishaela. "And what are you even doing-"

"Hello, Attendance Office?" Jaiden said then.

I'm scaring myself, I sound so good.

"Yes. What can I do for you?"

Jaiden could tell that it was that old scary-looking lady that worked in the office on the other end of the call. Part of the reason she had perfected this voice was because she'd rather call in as her mother and risk being found out than to be stared down by this woman. It was as if she took absences as a personal offense.

I don't know her name. I'm a freshman, okay? I can't know everyone's name.

"Yes, hello. This is Evelyn Winchester. My daughter, Jaiden, and her friend Mishaela Pagliardi, were involved in a minor accident last night that resulted in an overnight hospital stay and, to be cautious, they will not be at school today."

The silence following her statement was uncomfortable.

"Just today?"

"Ye— uh, that's as far as I know so far, ma'am. The school board requires me to call in every day anyway, so you'll hear from me again tomorrow if anything changes."

During the following silence, Jaiden silently thanked her father for mentioning that school board fact once during dinner.

"So was it a minor accident, or did it result in a hospital stay? Because those two things contradict each other. And why haven't we heard from Mishaela's parents? They do know they'll have to report in, as well."

This was going to take some thought. "Well, we're trying to get a hold of either of them, but you must realize that her father is a very busy corporate man, and her mother doesn't speak much English, so it's a work in progress. And maybe the accident wasn't minor at all, but heaven forbid I speak incorrectly while my child is in the hospital!"

This time, the silence was more pointedly tense than passively skeptical. Jaiden felt that this was appropriate; after all, if someone had been this prodding when she'd said her child had been in an accident, she'd be just as offended as she was projecting her mother to be.

"Right. I'm sorry to hear about the situation. At any rate, thank you for calling, Mrs. Winchester. I'll just need the girls' division numbers, and from there I'll be able to let their teachers know not to expect them today."

Jaiden knew her own division number, obviously, but she didn't know Mishaela's. However, after a split second, she realized that was fine, because Mishaela's mother wouldn't know it either; or her own mother, for that matter. "Oh, their division numbers?" she asked, making sure to turn up the confused inflection in her voice. "I don't really know. They're both in their first year. Does that help?"

"It does, actually."

"Does it?" She asked in disbelief.

I'm really pulling this off. Holy crap.

"Yes, I should be able to locate them with that. All I'll need is for both of them to bring a signed doctor's note upon their return to school, and to give it to their homeroom teachers."

Shit.

Wait a sec. Mishaela's dad has an office where he prints all sorts of official-looking things; I'm pretty sure a doctor's note could be one of those things. And if not, I'm equally sure there's some way we can scrounge something up to make it look official. Maybe her sister could help us, even. She's knowledgeable about that kind of thing.

"A doctor's note. I got it. Thank you so much. Bye now."

Jaiden hung up. "You can forge a doctor's note in your dad's office," she told Mishaela.

Mishaela gasped, covering her mouth. "You actually got away with it?!" she said.

Jaiden nodded. "For you. Don't say I've never done anything for you, kiddo. Now let's get going."

"To your house, right?" asked Mishaela, as they began to walk out of the restaurant.

"Yeah." Jaiden nodded. "Sometimes, if it's possible of course, it's helpful to go to the place the dream occurred– the 'scene of the crime,' if you will– to notice things you didn't before. That means we have to take a specific route: the same one from our dream."

They had a slightly longer walk since they had to avoid the school, but it was still a walkable distance. "But, they can track that number, can't they?" asked Mishaela, nervously pulling the hem of her dress. "And even if they don't, doesn't the school send an automated message when a student misses a day, regardless of if their parent calls in? I'm sure the person you spoke to already thought that call was highly suspect. We aren't getting out of this cleanly, you can be sure of that."

Jaiden stopped walking. "Mishaela Marzia Pagliardi, I order you to cut that out," she said, pointing a finger at her theatrically. "I did everything in my power. Literally, there is no better way I could've done this. Did you not hear that *amazing* performance I put on? And... and what are you so worried about, anyway? It's not like your parents believe in lectures, or hitting their children, or anything like that. I don't even think they know how to punish a child. Bold of you to assume you'd ever face any repercussions for this little stunt. You'll be fine." With that, she started back walking.

Mishaela took a tentative step forward. "But..."

"But nothing!" Jaiden rebutted with another dramatic point, continuing to walk. "Now, come on, walk faster so we can get to my place quicker. It's chilly, and my legs are starting to get tired."

"I- I guess you're right." Mishaela began to pick up the pace.

As they both approached the point where the encounter had happened in their dreams, the hairs on Jaiden's arms seemingly began to rise. Feeling as though something were definitely very *different* here, she stopped, and began to look around.

"What's wrong?" asked Mishaela.

"I can feel it," Jaiden said softly. "That woman's presence."

"Oh. Something does feel a little... off, now that you mention it," agreed Mishaela. "But how can you be so sure that it's that particular woman?"

"The same way I've been sure of everything else so far: I just have the feeling," replied Jaiden. It was a feeling she couldn't quite put words to, but it was similar to when one could feel a certain tension in the air. It was almost like the sensation of feeling watched, but with less urgency to find out where the watcher was; although, the urgency only increased the longer Jaiden didn't see the woman she was looking for.

"Show yourself, ya weirdo! I know you're here! Where are you..?!"

She was met with only silence.

Mishaela looked around again, visibly nervous. "Okay. In addition to your yelling possibly drawing attention to us now, I'm starting to feel very uncomfortable, so what if we just hurried on to your house and—"

Jaiden abruptly turned around then and pointed. "Oh! Right there near the stoop!"

Chapter Three

Unexpected Sources

Mishaela motioned as if she was going to scream, but luckily Jaiden was quick enough to cover her mouth so she wouldn't. They didn't need any more unnecessary attention drawn to themselves.

The silence was palpable as the woman walked over to the nearest stoop, adjusting the fabrics of her elegant burgundy sari with its floral embroidery patterns in gold, before taking a seat. Her face's expression was unreadable as she turned her gaze to the two teens.

"So, I've finally gotten the two of you together. How convenient."

Neither of them moved, feeling a mixture of shock and fright.

"W-what..." Jaiden was able to force out, "What do you want from us?"

"I can't be here long, so I cannot tell you everything." With a grand sweep of her arm, the motion making the golden threads of embroidery on her sari sparkle in the sunlight, she continued. "But I do believe I've made it quite clear that I require both of your assistance. I can't force you to join our cause. No, forced help is worse than no help at all, isn't it? It leaves things so... uninspired. But I will tell you this: that the lives, liberties, and ambitions of so many innocent people depend upon your help. Remember this, if you should decide to help: find the terrazzo."

And with another grand sweep of her arm, she seemingly vanished right before their eyes.

"Uh... what just happened?" Jaiden asked. "I have concerns. If that truly was the first time we've seen that woman in person, how did we see her in our dreams? And explain how she knows what she talked about then, too? And just *where* the hell did she *go*?! We need to get to my house, like, yesterday. I will officially go crazy if we don't start getting some answers here."

"I agree." Mishaela nodded. "We aren't very far now, so let's hurry on."

At Jaiden's house, she turned up the thermostat and made hot chocolate, so that she and Mishaela could warm up after being outside so long in the October chill. After all of that had been situated, she sat on the couch with Mishaela, handing her a mug of chocolate with marshmallows.

"Grazie," she said, although a bit distantly.

Jaiden gave her a reassuring smile. Mishaela's mother had moved to the US from Italy when she was around the girls' age, and her father was Italian-American, which is why the girls had an Italian last name. It wasn't unusual to hear Mishaela say Italian words sometimes, because of this, and at this point Jaiden had learned some of the basic vocabulary. With Mishaela's mother being an immigrant, and Jaiden having a Black mother and white father, it was like they were bound to become friends at some point, being the "different" ones in their predominantly white American suburb.

"Why does this lady want *our* help?" Jaiden asked then. "We're fourteen. People try their best to forget we exist at this age, you know? And now suddenly, here's someone who is not only fine with us existing and all, but wants our help? Claiming to need it, even?" She sighed. "It's weird... but maybe it'll become less weird when we dissect the whole encounter. Is there anything that sticks out to you from that whole debacle?"

"I can't say so," replied Mishaela. "Nothing we haven't touched yet, at least. The only thing I can recall at the moment is the overwhelming sense of fear. That somehow felt scarier than if we'd have gotten caught at school."

"Yeah, no kidding," agreed Jaiden. "I can't remember the last time I felt any fear of consequence from ditching class, but *that*... it was like... it was like when you hear someone in the other room when you know you're home alone, except ten times worse."

Both turned their attention toward the hallway leading to the kitchen then, realizing that the hypothetical Jaiden had just offered was just a little too close to their current situation for comfort. It remained quiet even then, though, so after a moment they decided it must be safe.

"Something does stick out to me, actually, the more I think about it," Jaiden said then. "What does 'terrazzo' mean, Mishaela? It sounds Italian."

"Mm-hmm." She nodded, and sat her mug on the table. "It is. It means 'terrace.'"

"Interesting. Know of any terraces around here?"

"Not off the top of my head, no." Mishaela reclined on the back of the couch, beginning to think. "But maybe if I think for a while longer, I'll get it."

"Yeah. I'll try to think, too," Jaiden said then. "You know, more food for thought: is it possible that 'Terrazzo' is the name of a business, rather than an actual terrace?"

"That's actually *very* possible," Mishaela agreed. "When you think about it, it's probably more likely than finding an actual terrace in such an urban area. Well, suburban, but you get what I mean."

"Yeah." Jaiden nodded.

"To lend even more credence to the second idea: there's also the fact that there is a sizable Italian community a little bit south of here," added Mishaela, a hand under her chin as she continued to think. "And it would make a lot of sense for an Italian-owned company to use an Italian word. Is your computer nearby? It would probably be easier to work through this if we could pull up something supplementary— a list of businesses in the area, or at the very least, a map."

Jaiden stood to go grab her laptop; she'd left it in the dining room, so it wasn't a long walk away. "Right. That's *exactly* why you're the brains of this operation, Mishaela. See, doesn't it make sense now that I had to pull you out of school with me to investigate this?"

Mishaela gave her a deadpan stare. "I still haven't forgiven you."

Jaiden just gave her a warm smile in response as she sat back on the couch, opening her laptop.

"Here we are. I'll put this in satellite view, on the off chance that we're looking for an actual terrace. That way, we can also search for businesses at the same time, and see how they look so we know what to look for when we go to the area."

"Right." Mishaela nodded. "Well, so far I'm definitely not exactly seeing any excess of greenery in the immediate area."

"Yeah..." Jaiden began to zoom in on the map, hoping it would reveal some possible solutions. "You said there's an Italian demographic in which direction? South, right?"

"South." Mishaela nodded. "The slightest bit southeast, actually. Right around the area over here."

"Gotcha." Jaiden zoomed in just a bit, to get more exact information on the area's buildings. "This area looks even less green, and I don't think the names of any of these nearby businesses are cutting it either. Oh! What about this? Do you think a flower shop would qualify as a terrace?"

"Ordinarily, I'd say no, but what's making you ask that?"

"Look." Jaiden pointed. "This place called Forest of Flowers is what's catching my eye. Look at how that looks from overhead. It certainly looks terrace-y."

"Yeah, you're right. It's certainly more green than anything in the area that isn't a public park," Mishaela pointed out.

"Maybe we should try it?" Jaiden suggested.

"Should we?" Mishaela asked in return. "This is only the first one... but it's not far, and I guess there is merit in wanting to go before it starts getting too late in the afternoon."

"Exactly," Jaiden pointed a finger. "Let's just go and check it out first. After we have some intel on the place, we can form a more concrete idea of what we're gonna do. Look, there's a '50s fast food restaurant on the other end of the block, so we can stop there and brainstorm after we're done checking the place out. I'll get us milkshakes. Chocolate for you?"

Mishaela smiled, and then nodded. Jaiden knew her so well. "Chocolate for me."

"It's empty," Jaiden said, as she and Mishaela investigated the exterior of the flower shop. "And not just the place, either. There don't seem to be people in this area in general right now. Why aren't any cars passing by? That is… it's really weird."

"Yeah." Mishaela nodded. "Almost eerie. Was it like this when we were on our way?"

Jaiden tried to think, but then realized she didn't remember— which was also very strange. It had been a twelve-minute walk at most, and she remembered locking up behind themselves and stepping out of the house. *Had* everything been this quiet for the entire twelve minutes?

"I don't remember, but I guess that makes it easier to investigate, though," pointed out Jaiden. "See anything interesting? At the moment, the only notable thing I see is the lack of humans around."

She trailed off upon hearing the jingle of the bells on a store's door opening.

"The door's unlocked," Mishaela noted, pushing the glass door again to demonstrate and making the bells sound again. "Shall we go in?"

Jaiden nodded, almost teasing Mishaela about breaking and entering (but didn't want to make her start panicking again and run the risk of ruining the entire investigation), and they walked into the flower shop. Immediately upon entry, the earthy aromas of flowers, of potting mix, and plant food permeated the air within the shop. Since it wasn't open for business, the only light entering the building was that which made it through the glass doors at the entrance, or one of the three windows in the main room, so the lighting was relatively dim. It was extremely quiet— one could hear every step they took on the terracotta brick floor, and neither of them were wearing heels.

"I don't think I've ever been here, and yet..." Jaiden slowly turned in a circle, taking in her surroundings: the vast arrays of peonies, tulips, pansies, ferns, and shrubs adorning every wall, table, and shelf within immediate view— to the point where she couldn't see what color the walls or shelves were; there was only green, plus the occasional burst of bright reds, oranges, and pinks. "I'm feeling this weird sense of deja vu. Do you feel that, Mishaela?"

"Well, the more I think about it, the more I realize I probably *have* been here, once or twice, with my mom and my sister..." Mishaela thought. "That being said: I, too, feel this sort of, say, familiarity with this place that a person usually wouldn't feel if they'd only been here a couple of times in their childhood, you know?"

"Yeah, I get it." Jaiden nodded. "I wonder why that is."

Mishaela started, "For now I'm getting a really strong feeling—"

"—that we need to go this way," both girls said at the same time, pointing deeper into the greenery of the shop, where the light became even more scarce.

"Lovely. I've always wanted to be a criminal," Mishaela said as she fell in line, following behind Jaiden. "First ditching school, then we have you impersonating your mom and eventually needing forgery to get us out of this mess; now trespassing, and let's not forget a possible breaking and entering charge if someone asks how we got in here—"

"Hey, that door was unlocked. This one was given to us free," Jaiden pointed a finger. "And stop worrying. We won't be in here long enough for anyone to catch us. I can feel it."

The two continued to walk, guided only by the strange sense of deja vu that lingered over both of them. As they walked further into the store, the taller shrubs and trees became more dense and plentiful, making it necessary to push aside a branch every now and then, as though the two really were walking through a forest. Their path was eventually interrupted by a large, wooden door that was highlighted by a few spotlights shining onto it. This door was painted in blue hues, as if to mimic the sea, and had vines growing all over it. Its doorknob was rusty and worn; it looked as if it hadn't been touched in years.

"This looks like something out of an RPG, and I really feel like that's supposed to be symbolic somehow," Jaiden said as she stared at the door. "Mishaela. Do you trust my judgment? Do you have any reason you'd doubt me, about this?"

She shook her head, twisting her mouth into a crooked smile. "I know I've been giving you a lot of grief about the situation, but I do trust you," she said. "I wouldn't be here if I didn't. So, that means there must be something up with this door, right?"

"Right. But if it really is like an RPG, doors like this usually indicate either some kind of, like... really big superboss, or at least something that's gonna be life-changing somehow. We'd better arm ourselves adequately," Jaiden looked around before noticing a gardening spade on the floor. It was small, but it was better than nothing; she handed it to Mishaela. "Just make stabby motions with it if you need to defend yourself."

"With a tiny shovel?" she asked.

"Hey, if it can break hardened soil by passively digging, who knows the damage it could cause with blunt force?" Jaiden asked, pulling out her house keys from her pocket and carefully gripping them in her left hand. "There. We are ready for the door. Although I guess we won't know anything for sure unless we open it, so I'll do the honors. Stand back; if anything happens to me, I'll need you to run and get help."

"Okay." Mishaela nodded obediently.

"Here we go." Jaiden placed her hand on the doorknob, inhaling and exhaling in an attempt to regulate her breathing. She had to stay calm; if she weren't calm, Mishaela would panic, and she had to keep her safe; as she'd been doing all these years they were friends.

"Let's do this. No turning back. And a-one, and a-two, and a three—"

Chapter Four

The Others

When Jaiden had opened the door, a potent gust of wind had blown, and there had been a surge of light, enough to temporarily blind both of the youths. When the tension had ceased, they found themselves standing before some type of conference room, dimly lit with acoustic guitar music playing softly. There was a long, polished oak wood table in the middle of the room, with many matching wooden chairs around it, and there were a few bookshelves and cabinets along the walls. This area felt completely unfamiliar; in fact, at the moment, it felt as though the only similarity between where they stood now and where they had previously been is that they were both devoid of people.

"As the saying goes, we are not in Kansas anymore," Jaiden said. She let out a breath she had forgotten she'd been holding, scraping her feet against the carpet as she and Mishaela walked into the room. "And still no signs of life at all. 'Kay. So, what the hell just happened, and where are we now? Some answers would be real great right now."

No sooner had she said that, the door behind them— the one they'd walked through to get to this room in the first place— slammed shut. The noise startled the duo, making them look back at the door. Mishaela immediately hurried to put her hand on the knob and twisted it, relieved to see the room from before.

"That's... I thought that... it's a relief to still be able to see that room. Glad to be wrong. I guess we can start by looking around for— ah!" Mishaela nearly fell over, startled by noticing someone sitting in a chair at the table.

"So nice of you to join us."

This time, the girls' mutual dream visitor wore a top that was a bit like a sari, but instead of wrapping around her like a dress, it only wrapped around her torso, like a shirt; it was a deep blue, almost indigo, with silver and rose gold accents, and with this she wore a pair of loose-fitting linen white pants. She nodded toward the chairs with a vaguely positive expression, inviting the girls to sit; and, feeling no malice, they did.

"Jaiden, Mishaela, it is a pleasure to finally be able to sit and speak with you for a time."

"Uh, sure." Jaiden nodded. "Pleasure's all ours, uh..."

"My name is Laelia, and you now find yourselves in my native village. Shall I anticipate your desire to know more about it?"

The two exchanged a glance. "Sure, might as well," replied Jaiden with a shrug.

"For years now, this village has suffered under a leader who is selfish, sadistic; robbing our land of all its prosperity. Not long ago— longer ago than the span of either of your lives, but not *very* long in the grand scheme of things, I assure you— the scene outside of this house was vastly different from what it is today. Although this is, and has always been, a desert, there was once prosperity. Many native plants lined our streets, streets that children played on freely. Our meals were plentiful and colorful. We were all a people filled with joy. But for many years, that has not been the case. This dictator has robbed us of our joy, our harvests... he has taken our former way of life and mangled it until it has become nigh unrecognizable. We have suffered for far too long; we have prayed for help, and those prayers have been answered in different forms, of which you are two of them."

"So... the reason we're here is because you want a revolution?"

Jaiden had now perked up. Revolutions were one of the biggest reasons she had ever bothered to learn history; she often said she was a real anarchist at heart, and she loved the idea of unjust government being overthrown, no matter how big or small– and overthrowing the US government was out of reach at the moment, so this could be a welcome missive.

Looks like this is turning out to be a pretty cool situation after all, even if it is kinda strange. Strange and barely believable, but I guess there's no harm in playing along for now. After all, it's not every day that a random suburban kid gets pulled out of their boring normal life to take part in something as grand as a revolution. This... this is almost a dream come true, really, when you think of it that way.

"That's what I like to hear!" she then said, putting her fist in the air. "We are *definitely* the ones you want."

Mishaela put her hand up. She didn't usually object to things that sounded this pertinent for fear of inconveniencing anyone, so whatever she had to say had to be important. "Miss Laelia, I'd love to help you and your people, but we're two fourteen-year-olds. And only one of us is exactly an honor student—" she turned to Jaiden— "no offense."

She said that all as one long thought; Mishaela tended to run her sentences together when she spoke English. (Jaiden thought it sounded like she did it in Italian too; she just wasn't fluent enough to be sure.)

"None taken," Jaiden replied, smiling. She didn't even *want* to be an honor student; she'd seen how high-strung it had made Mishaela become.

"It's just... my lovely friend here sees the idea of revolution in a positive light. And that's not necessarily wrong; the things that are brought about as a result of a revolution are often positive in nature. But I worry about the process to get there: of the almost completely inevitable reality of... of loss, of bloodshed, maybe even war."

"Ah." Jaiden nodded. "I guess she does have a point. Even if the chances are slim that all of this is even real, slim doesn't mean zero, which means the idea of us getting hurt or worse is also non-zero, huh?"

"If I may address all your points at once?"

Both turned back to Laelia, surprised she was ready to speak so soon. "Yeah, go for it," Jaiden replied.

"Yes, you are young," Laelia agreed. "But are all revolutionists not young? If not by physical age, then in spirit? The ones who bring forth ideas of change and evolution are usually of the younger generation, you know. The very idea of a revolution is itself intertwined with themes of growth, of rebirth, which are also themes present with the particular coming of age you're likely accustomed to as teenagers." She turned to Mishaela. "Do not slight yourself. You are special; there is a reason the goddesses have ordained you for this task."

At this point, Mishaela and Jaiden were both blankly staring, as Laelia continued to speak.

"And if that does not instill confidence in you, rest assured that you will not be the only two people working to finally bring our unjust leader down. The allies you will come to know will be as dedicated to your safety as they will to the cause. Down the hall there are your quarters, where you'll also find various provisions to utilize during your stay. This building is where you'll be staying during the planning phase, so for now, remember it well. There is a possibility that you'll have to move bases as your plans progress, but I suppose you can face that later if it comes to pass. It is best that you use your own cunning to devise your plans, after all. With that, I do believe I've given you everything you need to begin planning to finally liberate this unfortunate place."

"Okay. If you could humor me for a second, how long do you expect us to—?"

Before Jaiden could get the sentence out, Laelia was already gone.

"How in the hell does she do that?" Jaiden asked then, with a huff. "I've gotta stop blinking when she's around."

"Well, *that* happened." Mishaela sighed, slumping in her chair. "What do you make of all this? It's a lot to take in at once, isn't it?"

"Yeah." Jaiden turned, finally noticing that the door the girls had arrived in had vanished at some point, and doing a double-take. "What the?!"

This made Mishaela turn as well, and she immediately tensed. "The door?!"

"It was right there, right? I'm not losing my mind here?" Jaiden asked.

"It was right there! I even, I almost thought it was gonna shut and then be unopenable from this side, so that's why I opened it from this side to be sure. It— this is the first time I feel so awful about being proven right, and I don't like it," Mishaela said. "How are we going to get back? It's one thing for the door to have shut or gotten stuck, but it's completely gone! You can't go back through a door that doesn't exist! What's the plan now, mastermind?"

Although Jaiden was quiet, she was just as worried as Mishaela was. If they'd be gone for a few hours that was one thing, but if she got home too late, her mother would create a spectacle of epic proportions, and she *really* didn't want that. "Okay, give me a minute and I can absolutely come up with a plan for this."

There was a short silence before Mishaela asked, "You have no idea what we should do, do you?"

"I don't know, I can't exactly consult the 'disappearing door' files in my brain," replied Jaiden.

"I shouldn't have come here. I should not be here." Mishaela curled into a ball in her chair, putting her head under her arms. "This isn't happening. This is not happening. I'll wake up and be in third period, and everything will be fine."

Another silence. "How can you wake up in third period? You never fall asleep in school."

"Well, what else am I supposed to believe?!" Mishaela asked frantically.

"Hey! I just had a thought. What if the door didn't disappear? What if it just... moved?" Jaiden asked.

"Moved?" Mishaela asked.

"Right." Jaiden hoisted her bag over her shoulder. "Let's survey the place and see if we can find either the door itself, or some clues pointing to it."

Mishaela couldn't find a reason to object to this— especially since she was already in so deep— so she found herself once again falling in line behind Jaiden as they proceeded. They began to walk down the first identifiable hallway, which had dark, bare wooden walls. "You're awfully calm about this," Mishaela noted.

"I'm always calm. You know this." Jaiden replied. "Are *you* done practically having a panic attack over this?"

Mishaela looked around. "For some strange reason, I'm feeling this sensation of… is familiarity a good word? Not as if I've been here, because I know I haven't, but more like… like this reminds me of somewhere that I *have* been before. Somewhere that would be a distant memory by now, but a place that I know was safe. And that feeling makes it feel like this isn't a dangerous place, at least."

"Yeah. Got it." Jaiden nodded, and turned to a wooden brown door— just to notice that it was already partially cracked.

Is someone else here? She thought to herself.

"What's wrong?" asked Mishaela, noticing her hesitation.

Jaiden put a finger up to her lips, to signal to be quiet, before carefully nudging the door open.

Within the room's eggshell-tinted walls were three bunk beds in an otherwise minimally decorated area. There were no frames or posters decorating the walls, and the only other furniture that seemed to be around were two bare end tables and a wooden chair, all seeming to be made of the same mahogany. Although all of the beds were fitted with sky blue sheets, two of the beds weren't quite as neat as the other four, indicating that there were two other people already staying there.

"Who's there?" called a feminine voice, coming from the direction of the other door in the room (presumably a closet).

"Oh my god. Madeline?" Jaiden said when she noticed who the girl was.

Madeline Navarro was in her second year at the same school that Jaiden and Mishaela attended. She was within their same height range, if not a bit taller, and had dark brown eyes with light brown hair that fell to the middle of her back and fair skin, her build more toned than the other two due to being a competitive figure skater. She currently wore a simple gray long-sleeved dress. Whenever Jaiden had seen her around school, it wasn't unusual for it to be with Mishaela; their parents had all been classmates when they'd been in high school, so they'd practically known each other from birth. In addition to that, Madeline played cello in the school's orchestra, and Mishaela played violin.

"Well, isn't this a small world?" Madeline said upon seeing the duo. "Jaiden, Mishaela. I certainly wasn't expecting to see anyone I knew here, but I guess it's comforting at the same time."

"I'll say. How long have you been here?" Mishaela asked, just as surprised.

"Just a day and a night," Madeline replied, tucking a piece of her hair behind her ear. "I bet my parents are really worried about me, though. I haven't been able to call them and tell them I'm okay. As a matter of fact, my phone died the minute I arrived here."

That prompted Mishaela and Jaiden to look at both of theirs.

"Yep. They're dead too." Mishaela nodded.

"Well, things have officially gotten real," Jaiden said. "I know for a *fact* that my battery wasn't low; I specifically charged it right before we left my house, just in case things got sketchy when we were trying to see what was going on."

They didn't get a chance to drive that train of thought any farther, because it was then that the other occupant of the room walked in. She was the shortest of the group so far, and had long, full brown hair, even longer than Mishaela's; it could easily touch her hips. She was wearing a maroon off-shoulder ribbed sweater with a black shirt underneath, and blue jeans. "Oh, now it's a party," she said dryly, moving her bangs away from her dark brown eyes. "You must be the others that we've been told to wait for. Jasiela, by the way."

"Nice to meet you," Jaiden said. "Jaiden here. This is my best friend, Mishaela."

Mishaela waved amiably. "Hi," she said, smiling.

"Hi," Jasiela replied, smiling back in a way that didn't feel quite as kind. She sat on the bottom bunk opposite the one Jaiden had mentally claimed. "I might not sound excited, but I really am glad you guys are here. It's been so *boring* just sitting here all the time, but this one—" she gestured toward Madeline— "insisted that *no*, we had to wait for more of you guys. Maybe now we can finally get a move on things."

"She's been here exactly three hours," Madeline muttered, before she shook her head. "I wouldn't be so hasty. When I spoke with Laelia, she said there's a total of five. That means one more before we can officially start the revolt that's been hinted at."

"We have the people behind us already?" Jaiden asked, impressed. "The most important factor in a revolution is having the majority of the populace in favor of it, you know. How'd you get that done in a day and a half?"

"I think it's safe to say that that was put into place long before I got here. Have you *seen* the people around here?" Madeline countered. "Hell yeah, they're behind us already! You'd be too, if you had to live like they do. Actually, maybe we should be setting out to find dinner. If we all go together, you can get a change of scenery, Jasiela, and it'll be a good way for you all to understand the situation a little better." She walked back over to the closet on the far side of the room, and opened the door before pulling out a wooden chest.

"By the way, something I found out about this place is that you're required to wear some pretty conservative clothing, for now at least, due to laws about clothing restrictions. We don't want to draw any unnecessary attention, you know what I mean?"

"Can they at least be colorful?" asked Mishaela.

"Yeah, sure. There's a bunch of stuff in here," replied Madeline, opening the chest to reveal brightly colored fabric with brilliant shiny and sparkling details, as well as darker colors, and minimally decorated silks.

"Oh, these are gorgeous!" Jasiela picked up a dark pink silk with gold detailing, a geometric pattern that sparkled under the lighting in the room.

"My thoughts exactly!" agreed Mishaela, picking up a dark green piece of fabric and examining it, smiling when she noticed the small jewel-like stones sewed onto it in a floral pattern. The blue, pink, and purple jewel tones contrasted brilliantly against the fairly dull green. "I think this might be some type of sari-like thing. Madeline, you've done this before, right? Could you give me a hand?"

"Sure!" Madeline clapped her hands, grinning, while Mishaela just gave her a deadpan stare.

She did go over to help, though. After they were adequately suited up, everyone's eyes fell on Jaiden, still struggling with her fabric.

"What? Have you actually tried to wear a sari? It's not easy." She was clearly embarrassed, a tinge of pink on her cheeks.

"What do you mean, have we tried? We're literally wearing them right now," pointed out Jasiela.

Jaiden frowned, and pointed a finger. "Now, look here—"

"Will you ever learn to ask for help, Jaiden?" Mishaela said then, sounding more like a disappointed parent than a childhood friend, as she and Jasiela helped Jaiden out of her tangled mess of fabric.

"You might wanna just get something else," added Jasiela. "It'd take a while to untangle that."

"Yeah, yeah..." Jaiden mumbled, already reaching for a more simple black cloak. It matched her current mood, after all.

"If we're all ready now?" asked Madeline. "I'd like to get back as soon as possible. Everyone, follow me; the market is a short walk away."

Outside, the landscape that awaited the quartet was devoid of any greenery, life, and sound. It was eerily quiet, and the building they'd come from seemed to be the only one around until they would arrive at the main town area. It was as Laelia had said: clearly a desert, but one completely barren of any personality.

"This whole place... can you say depressing?" Jaiden said softly to herself. "Nothing is here. Nothing is living. It's awful."

"I'm confused. Where does everyone live?" asked Mishaela. "Yes, I see that there are buildings ahead of us. But it doesn't seem like there are that many, especially when you factor in the possibility of businesses, restaurants, a schoolhouse, things such as that."

"Oh. I didn't even think of that, but you know what..." Madeline hummed. "That's a good point. I only know a little more than you guys do, and I never thought to ask about the education system here. But something I did notice— speaking of a lack of buildings— is that there definitely are more people than there are houses for them. It's not the best of situations."

The group had arrived in town now, and were immediately met with a couple of guards. They were outfitted in mulberry-colored uniforms consisting of bomber jackets and loose pants, and a sash over their shoulders, assumedly different depending on their rank because one guard had a red one, and the other, light gray. Both also held nightsticks in their hands, as if ready to use them at any time. One held his hand up, wordlessly, motioning for them to stop; the other had a brief look over the group of four just as silently before waving them in.

"Hm. Considering that search wasn't in-depth enough to detect any concealed weapons or substances, I wonder what exactly they're looking for," Jaiden said softly, but no one replied.

They had now come across the outdoor market; but that wasn't the reason conversation had halted.

Jasiela pointed to the gigantic building at the north end of town. Its base structure was a terracotta orange color, and it had organic designs all around it in a dark red color. Its roof convened into a pointed dome, striped in an orange-tinted cream and dusty yellow. There were several other domes as well, but none as tall as the central one. "I'm gonna take a wild guess here. That's where the enemy lives?"

"Yep." Madeline nodded. "You got it."

"Not very covert, is he?" asked Mishaela, straightening her glasses. "The design is impressively detailed, but it's not very original; it bears a resemblance to a particular famed Indian architecture."

"I'll say." Jaiden agreed. "It's too bad the guy's apparently— and pretty obviously— evil, because the building itself is actually pretty nice. But I will say: it *is* a bit much against the surroundings."

The four were silent for a moment before continuing into the marketplace, denoted by a large green, orange, and yellow striped flag flying over the area. In this area, many wooden outdoor stands were situated in such a way that they created aisles, not too much unlike a grocery store or farmer's market. There were many things on offer today, from soup to sweets, but Jaiden noticed almost immediately that she didn't see any meat for sale.

Hm. That sounds familiar, doesn't it? Except instead of there being no beef like in my dream that time, there's no meat at all.

"Okay, everyone," Madeline called everyone else to attention. "I don't think any of us want to spend more time here than we need to. We can get this done efficiently if we split up. How about this: I'll find fruit and spices. Jaiden, you get some vegetables. Jasiela, you're in charge of rice and grains, and Mishaela, you can get some nuts, as in peanuts. Anybody got any objections or anything?"

"Not an objection, but a question on veggies?" asked Jaiden. "I've never been very big on them, so I don't know what to grab. Suggestions?"

"In that case, the two of us can stick together," replied Madeline. "I would just grab some spinach leaves, broccoli, and corn, because you can never go wrong with any of those; but seeing them in person helps, especially to see if they're fresh. If that's all, then everyone, meet here in like... fifteen minutes so we can pay for everything."

Madeline and Jaiden arrived at the fruit stands first, since they were closest to the market's entrance. As Madeline carefully studied a batch of cranberries, Jaiden looked around– a bit curious, but mostly just trying to place where in the world they could be. Surely, this town didn't really evoke imagery of any particular place she'd read about in her (very many) history books; it felt more like a conglomerate of many of them. She did notice, in relation to Mishaela's question earlier about where everyone lived, that many of the buildings here had multiple levels. The nearest one at present looked like it was both a school and some type of clothing store, so there was probably no such thing as individual houses– not to mention, none of the buildings looked to be in particularly good shape. They'd aged; not too much unlike the building that Jaiden, Mishaela, and Madeline normally went to school in.

Jaiden and Madeline's attention was then diverted by the screech of a small child piercing the air.

"I want candy!" they screamed, reaching for one of the stalls with one of their hands. The other was being desperately pulled by the adult with them, presumably their mother.

"We can get candy next time, when your father comes back," she said in a voice that was clearly hushed. "Now come on, let's go home and eat what we got today–"

"NO! Candy!" the child screamed, making the mother wince. The child was crying now, and as she noticed one of the guards from earlier approaching, Jaiden was suddenly filled with an overwhelming sense of dread.

She turned to Madeline, and realized she had felt it too. "I am getting a really bad feeling," she said softly.

"What is this noise?" the guard asked, in a low but resonating voice.

"I-it's nothing," the mother quickly stuttered, pulling even more frantically at her child's arm. "We were just on our way home, actually..."

"No! I want candy!" the child insisted, screaming to a volume that pierced the ears of everyone in the immediate area.

Jaiden turned away, wincing, in the nick of time to avoid seeing the child get struck with the guard's nightstick. "You will be silent!" he said, not satisfied with just one strike, amidst the child's cries and the mother's pleas to stop.

"Please stop! He doesn't know what he's doing! Please don't– strike me instead!" the mother continued to plead. "I can't lose this child too!"

Perhaps just as unnerving as the currently unfolding scene between the guard, the mother, and the child was that those closest to the excursion— among them a few forms that were certainly larger and possibly stronger than the guard— merely looked on, or averted their eyes as well. Was there no solidarity in this town? Surely there were enough of them to overpower the one guard.

"That's so awful," Madeline said softly, with tears in her eyes. "That's just a kid! They can't be older than five, based on their size."

"It's horrible!" agreed Jaiden. "I can't imagine what they do to insubordinate *adults*, if that's what they do when a kid is having a temper tantrum. I have to—"

"No." Madeline put an arm out to stop Jaiden from doing anything reckless. "Those guys are buff and armed, and there's two of them. It's not an exaggeration when I say: you doing anything to intervene would be suicide."

Jaiden sighed in exasperation. She knew Madeline was right, as much as she didn't want her to be.

"Anyway, can we cut this short? I don't want to be in this area longer than I have to— wait, is that a cantaloupe?" she asked, casting a look at the round fruit Madeline had been studying, and was now holding in her hands. "Madeline, you can't get a cantaloupe. Mishaela's allergic; it turns her skin all red. You know this." Jaiden took it from her and put it back, and picked up a honeydew melon. "Here. Use this instead, it's safe."

She raised her eyebrows in surprise. "Okay, yeah, thanks for reminding me of that; it slipped my mind. All the, uh, recent alien mind tricks or whatever is happening here must've left me all scrambled."

"No problem. I wonder if Mishaela and Jasiela have had any luck," Jaiden said then. "I know we had a meeting spot all set up and all, but do you think we should go look for them?"

"Let's. The sooner we get out of here the better," replied Madeline, clearly still shaken up by the events that had transpired not too long ago.

Once everyone had gathered and the food was paid for, and as everyone started the trip back to the base, Jasiela asked, "So where does a big bad guard guy get off beating a literal child? I already hate it here. Like, more than I did before."

"What I don't get is that there were so many people in the area, including quite a few big guys. But they were all just standing there," Jaiden replied. "What was their problem? They would've easily had the manpower to overtake that guy. Where's the care for their fellow man?"

"Hm. While that's true, remember the entrance to the market area?" Jasiela asked. "There were three or four guards posted there. Not to mention that the palace was pretty close to there. Assuming that's where most of the guards are posted, it's probably a death sentence to try to overpower one guard in that kind of situation."

Just like Madeline had said. "Ah." Jaiden sighed. "Everything you just said makes perfect sense, but I still don't like it."

"I just hope we never have to see anything like that ever again," Mishaela added softly, her hands clasped tightly together. For a child who had never been privy to corporeal punishment, it was easy to understand why this was affecting her so strongly. Jaiden and Madeline knew this, and both started to try and think of a way to change the subject to calm her down.

Jaiden asked then, "Is there no meat here? I didn't see any at that market."

"No, there's meat," Jasiela said. "I saw some while we were there on the far end of the stands. But we've been told that those specific markets are all run by the dictator, and because of that the picks are slim at best. Sounds about right because everything I saw was mostly fat. I don't know about you guys, but to me, bad meat is worse than no meat at all."

She then lowered her voice, and continued: "Laelia mentioned to us that there are a group of rebels that live by the river that know we're here, and they send fish to the house we're living in periodically, to share with us. Catching fish for sustenance is technically illegal here from what I hear, but hey, I guess they don't care about that. And now that I think about it, why should they? They're rebels."

"Ah, right, plus there wouldn't be any beef here anyway," Jaiden added. "Assuming— based on the climate, the common attire, and the architecture— we're where we most likely should be, cows are worshiped here; I learned that in World Studies."

"We're *not* in India." Madeline stopped walking and turned to her companions. "You guys, to directly address the elephant in the desert: this place isn't like any place I've ever been to, seen, or even heard of. It looks too... different. It even *feels* different, you know? And we're definitely not still at home." She gestured toward the market. "But of course you knew that. Does this look like Chicago to you?"

Jasiela gasped. "You're... from Chicago." She looked confused.

"Well, Jaiden and I live in suburbs adjacent to the main metropolitan area. But for the sake of continuity within this conversation: yes, we do." Mishaela turned her head slightly sideways. "This seems to be a surprise to you. Do you not usually live in the Chicago area?"

"No. Not even close. I live in Spanish Harlem," Jasiela said, slightly breathless.

It was the others' turn to be shocked. "Spanish Harlem?" Madeline repeated. "Like New York City, Spanish Harlem?"

Jasiela nodded. "That's the one. So... that being the case... where the hell are we *now*?"

"Well, if this conversation is telling us anything, it's that we obviously have a lot more to learn about this place," Jaiden said. "Why don't we get settled in at our base of operations, and then worry about this? It'll be easier to think when we're all sitting down and eating. I don't know about you guys, but I'm practically starving here."

"Agreed," Madeline nodded. "By the way, speaking of cooking, if anyone wanted to help me cook, I was thinking of making the fish with a cranberry glaze."

"That sounds delicious!" Mishaela agreed. "The nuts would add a nice crunch, too. But how were you planning on preparing the fish?"

"Good question! So that's gonna depend on the kind of fish I end up using tonight," replied Madeline. "You see, there's a few different types of fish that are native to this area. I dunno what any of them are called, but one of them is really good when you grill it, but one is more dry, and needs to be either sauteed or broiled. I know there's some butter in the fridge, so I could use that."

"Oh, a nice crisp on the edges would be just divine," added Jaiden. "I think it'd be best to use the drier fish, because then the sauce can hydrate it. Now, are we using the honeydew tonight?"

The group continued to discuss dinner plans as they walked back to their base. Madeline made sure to glance at Mishaela periodically, and she thankfully seemed a lot less tense than she had been a few minutes prior. Hopefully, this would be the last time any of them would have to witness a scene like they had in the marketplace.

Chapter Five

Gavin and the Resistance

U pon their return, the four teenagers were not even able to put their groceries away before noticing that something was amiss in the house.

"...Hey, does it feel like someone was here while we were gone?" Madeline was the first to ask.

"*That's* what this feeling is!" Jaiden snapped her fingers. "I was having trouble putting words to it. It's like, nothing was moved, but you can feel that something's just... different from when we'd left."

"Are you guys *sure* you aren't just being paranoid?" Jasiela asked, the skepticism in her voice overflowing in her words.

"No, no, I feel it as well," agreed Mishaela. "There's a certain... presence about."

"Right. Okay. Sure." Clearly, Jasiela was still not a believer— but it was then that the four heard the sound of motion in the kitchen. The subsequent sounds of footsteps caused all four of them to visibly tense up.

"But... we locked the doors," Mishaela whispered.

"Yeah. We did. But honestly, this place is weird enough that ghosts don't sound out of the ordinary," Jaiden pointed out. Indeed, after saying that, she felt a chill go down her spine, and shivered. "You have to be careful when dealing with ghosts. We need a plan. We need—"

She turned around, narrowly missing bumping heads with a teenage boy about her height. His wavy hair, of a warm shade of pecan brown, was cut short at the sides, but reached his ears from the crown of his head, neatly brushed to his right; his fair skin with pink undertones and crystalline cerulean blue eyes were a combination that easily distinguished him from the rest of the people in the house so far.

"Whoa!" Jaiden stumbled back, startled; midway through her fall feigning getting into an improvised karate pose, and regaining her footing with her arms in a martial arts-inspired stance. "Stay back! I am perfectly trained in the ancient art of whoop-ass!"

The boy laughed softly, amused by her antics. "Please don't be frightened; I don't intend to cause any harm."

The sound of his voice, once again, sent everyone else into a state of confusion. Perhaps there was a contrast in Jasiela's phrasing or minor differences in her vocabulary, due to her being from a different part of the US than Madeline, Jaiden, and Mishaela. And perhaps they all had speech patterns that were different still, due to their cultural differences. But this young gentleman's accent itself was striking to all four of them. Not even his fashion sense had hinted at a different nationality; he had kind of a rockabilly style, wearing a red-and-white checkered short-sleeved shirt and loose blue jeans. Hearing him speak had stunned all four of them.

"Um... how can I say this..." Madeline whispered to Jasiela and Mishaela. "He is... obviously *not* from either Chicago or New York."

"Yeah, no shit, the British accent gives it away," agreed Jasiela.

"Sorry, your accent kinda took us all by surprise," she apologized then for the somewhat uncomfortable silence.

He nodded, indicating he took no offense. "Understood. Well, then... I'm Gavin," he introduced himself, smiling, and placing his hands into his pockets. "I'll be staying here— and working with— the four of you, as the situation has been explained to me; does that align with... your expectations?"

After a short silence, Madeline said, "Well, there was never any word about what the fifth person would be like, just that five of us would be here. There are five of us here now, so I guess it does!"

"Wonderful. I'm actually happy to find out I'll be working with four girls. I've tried to do things with other boys, and they're absolute rubbish at teamwork; I mean, whether it's at home or at school, I can't tell you how many times a perfectly good plan has been ruined by—" He looked at everyone timidly. "Oh, I'm sorry. I didn't mean to ramble."

"Uh-huh." Jasiela was the first to speak. "Well, then, introductions, right? I'm Jasiela. This is Mishaela, Madeline, and the one who went all kung-fu on you is Jaiden. Welcome aboard; it sounds like you've had things explained to you, at least," she held out her hand.

Gavin took this moment to shake hands with everyone. "That's right. Everything was explained to me by this strange woman who guided me here, and whilst there are some minor details I'm still a bit confused about, I do believe I have a sufficient understanding of the core issue here. More or less. Er, for the time being though, might I help you with dinner, then?" he asked, pointing to the groceries.

"Oh! Of course," Madeline said. "I'm in charge of dinner. Follow me."

For dinner, Madeline and Gavin worked together to prepare sauteed fish with vegetables and almonds in a sweet sauce. After dinner was done cooking, everyone sat on the floor of the main bedroom to eat and discuss the matter at hand.

"All right, if we're starting a discussion, then let's start with the main thing I don't think we can avoid anymore," Madeline said. "None of us knows where we are."

"Not only that," Jaiden added, "we seem to have arrived here from places all over the world; not by way of plane or anything, but by walking through a door, as if we were just going into another room."

"There's also that strange, foreign feel in the air, and the fact that no one's phones seem to work here. Come to think of it, I haven't even seen anyone with a phone here either." Madeline closed her eyes and exhaled in frustration. "It's almost like we've traveled back in time."

"What do you call it when there's a place that can't be explained?" Jasiela asked rhetorically.

There was a brief silence then, everyone pondering this.

Even if science is a subject I'm horrible at, I just can't wrap my head around any of this.

But I'm beginning to think that science doesn't play a part in this, the more I sit and simmer on it. A woman who's able to transcend the lines between dreams and reality? A mysterious transporting door that brought teenagers here from different places all over the world? This place... in general?

Nothing about that sounds scientific at all. Impossible, if you really think about it. But even if it's impossible, somehow, it still happened.

Jaiden gasped. "Okay, guys, I know this may sound crazy," I said, "but hear me out. Keep an open mind here. I have a thought about all of this. Do you think this all could be... magic?"

This claim was met by silence, but no one refuted it.

"Magic?" repeated Jasiela. "Seriously? That's the best you could come up with?"

Never mind.

"Yeah, it is, actually," Jaiden said, defending herself. "Think about it. We didn't get into a car, or on a train, or a plane, or anything like that. We didn't walk here, either. Even if we had, the amount of time we spent getting here is impossible with any of those methods. Teleporting is pretty impossible, as far as I know."

"We should also keep in mind that, even disregarding the method of transportation, the order in which we got here doesn't make any logical sense," added Mishaela. "Madeline got here more than a day before Jaiden and I, and we live close enough together that we all attend the same school; yet we got here the same day that Gavin did, who logically would've been here much later considering there would be a whole ocean to get over somehow."

"But magic isn't real." Madeline said that, but there was something in her voice that showed she wasn't entirely convinced of her own words.

"Then, would anyone else like to offer any different explanations?" Jaiden asked. "My ears are ready for you to lay them on me."

The room went silent, excluding the sounds of dinner being eaten.

"But—" Jasiela started, but trailed off.

More silence.

"...There... isn't any other way to explain it, really," Gavin spoke up. "Believe me, a *very* large part of me wants to be able to refute what you just said with any shred of evidence I could muster, but there is none. Then again, I suppose I have only been here about two hours at most."

"Gavin's got a point, I guess," agreed Madeline. "Besides, we didn't even have control over where we ended up. If we did, I sure as hell wouldn't have ended up in a place like this, I can tell you *that*."

"Oh, guys?" Mishaela waved her hand timidly, as if the congregation was in school instead of... wherever they were. "I just noticed something interesting. When Jaiden and I walked through that door and arrived here, it was still early. Enough time has passed here for us to, at the very least, take a walk and eat a meal, right?"

"Right," Madeline agreed.

"Look at this."

Mishaela showed everyone the screen of her iPod. It read: 9:41 a.m. Everyone reacted to this revelation, whether it be a soft gasp or a stare of disbelief.

"Can I see that?" Jasiela asked.

"Certainly." Mishaela nodded, and surrendered her iPod.

"Hmm. Yeah, it is set to Central time..." Jasiela was thinking. "But it's dark outside here now. And... there is apparently absolutely no wifi around here."

"No wifi?" Gavin looked horrified. "At all? What kind of terrible place is this?!?"

The others all laughed at Gavin, even though he was being completely serious.

"So... magic?" asked Madeline. "Well, that or aliens—"

"Magic," Jaiden and Mishaela both immediately replied. They knew to stop Madeline before she got to talking about aliens. It would only give way to more conspiracy theories...

"So we're just going with this now. Nice." Jasiela folded her arms.

"Well, what do *you* want us to do?" asked Jaiden. "Even if we're wrong, I think it's safe to assume we have no way of leaving this place until we find out how to help these people with their problems, because we have no way of knowing where we even are just yet. What's the point of getting that caught up in the specifics anyway? Let's just put it on the backburner until it's something that's on a, like, need-to-know, life-or-death basis."

"I suppose you're correct," agreed Gavin.

"I guess..." replied Jasiela.

"Exactly. So now that we can consider that out of the way," Jaiden said, taking a sip of water. "Let's discuss some other things. Hmm... there is the fact that we don't know how long we're gonna be here, so— especially for those of us that are new to each other— we might as well get better acquainted, right? We already know each other's names, so... how old is everybody?"

"Fifteen," Madeline said. "I think I'm still the oldest, right? Gavin?"

"If this rests upon my answer, you are. I'm fourteen." He looked at the remaining three. "And you all?"

"Also fifteen," Jasiela said.

"We're both fourteen," Jaiden said. "So with the exception of Madeline, we're all freshmen in high school, correct?"

"Not correct, I'm in my second year," replied Jasiela.

"I'm in my first year of secondary school, yes," added Gavin.

"I think," Mishaela said, "that where Gavin is from, they call it being a Year Nine. Is that correct?"

"It is," Gavin said, looking a bit impressed. "How do you know that?"

"Well, for starters, my mom is European. Italian, to be exact. But I've been told, also, that I'm kind of a brain." Mishaela smiled at Jaiden. "Right?"

"Oh, yeah," she agreed. "She gets to school early just to read in our library. Total brain."

Gavin laughed lightly at Jaiden's confirmation of Mishaela's nerdery. "You two seem to be quite close; you must have known each other even before now, then?" he asked.

"Yeah," Mishaela said. "She's my best friend, actually. Madeline goes to school with us, too; we all live in the Chicago area."

"I'm from New York," Jasiela added. "What about you?"

"London." Gavin thought, and then said, "It seems that one similarity between all of us— aside from our ages— is that we've come from big cities."

Jaiden resisted the urge to correct Gavin about her and Mishaela's tiny suburbs, deciding him not knowing was of no consequence.

"You know, it's interesting that we've been able to settle into a routine that's so much different than usual, so quickly," Madeline said then. "Personally, I feel that it's a little more comfortable than waking up so early to go to school, but... even so, you'd think there'd be more of an adjustment period. It's really curious."

"It is, isn't it?" agreed Mishaela. "What's more, usually with waking up for school comes that regular feeling of sluggishness around 3 p.m. I haven't felt that since we've been here, either."

"How very *interesting*." Madeline placed her hands in her lap, pondering.

The room fell silent then, as everyone finished their dinner. One could hear the sounds of nighttime outdoors: the wind blowing through the boughs of the intermittent barren trees, the shifting sands, and the calls of the native nocturnal bugs that sounded foreign to all five of their senses. If it wasn't still so hot outside, it might have been a good evening to sit and absorb the atmosphere.

"I can tell you guys one thing," Jasiela said, "this place is *way* quieter than *my* house is. I have my parents, three sisters, three brothers, and my grandparents all living in the same house. It's nuts. I think the only time I ever get any peace and quiet is when everyone else has gone to bed for the night."

"I bet," Jaiden concurred. "I have older siblings, but they're all grown up; I'm the only one that still lives with Mom and Dad. But even so, there's only four of us total, six including my parents, so if we all lived together it still wouldn't get quite *that* crazy."

Although vaguely, Jaiden could remember those days when her older siblings still lived at home. She remembered how loud the house got around dinnertime: buzzing, full of energy and conversation about the days that everyone had had, or what was yet to come. Sometimes, rarely, it would be so loud that it would be difficult to hear her own thoughts; but even so, even reminiscing on it now she felt a bittersweet feeling. While she didn't exactly want her siblings back home, she still kind of missed them.

Madeline spoke next. "I have a pair of younger twin sisters. They're also freshmen at school; I think..." she pointed a finger at

Jaiden hesitantly. "Jaiden, you're pretty good friends with Cristina, right?"

"Yeah, she's cool," Jaiden told her. Jaiden was actually wearing Cristina's shoes right now; that's why they were too small. She was a half size smaller than Jaiden was, and that usually didn't matter. Usually.

"I only have one sibling," Mishaela said. "My older sister, Chiara. She and I are really close, though."

"Chiara is, if you can believe it, a bigger brain than Mishaela," Jaiden added. "She's also really quiet, too, though."

But the real treat was what would happen if one got Chiara to trust them enough that she was no longer as quiet around them. When that happened, they'd be in for fascinating takes on what one would consider some of the most mundane aspects of life. Chiara had the most interesting ideas about the reasons that fruit fell from the tree at the specific time it did, or why fireflies lit up at the frequency they did, or why socks seemed to get lost in the dryer.

Actually, now that Jaiden was thinking about this... her explanations often involved a certain level of belief in magic too, didn't they?

Gavin then told his new companions of his home back in London; that it was filled with the noise of his three younger brothers being rowdy, and that he and his sister were the quieter ones.

"My brothers are right annoying. They always tease me about everything: like the fact that my favorite color is purple, or that I eat a lot, or that— as they say— I'll never have a girlfriend because I'm too shy." Gavin frowned. "I don't think I'm shy. Besides, the implication that someone should change the way they are for the sake of attracting others is an awful one indeed. And just for the sake of argument, I happen to think that there are some girls who would like shyness in a male partner."

"Of course they would!" Jasiela smiled. "It's a really desirable trait for some people. Hardly anyone likes loud guys. They tend to be rude. Misogynist. Hygiene is probably lacking." Jaiden nodded, agreeing.

Gavin laughed. "I suppose so," he agreed. "Well, it's getting late, or at least I assume it's getting late, so I'll get on to bed now. See you all tomorrow."

"Lucky, Gavin gets his own room," Madeline complained. "Nah, I'm just messing with you. Come on, I'll show you where the other bedrooms are."

"Good night!" Jaiden said, as she and Mishaela waved.

"Good night. Bright and early, then?" asked Gavin.

"...can we do bright and kinda early, but not really?" asked Jasiela. "I'm just saying, if this is gonna be a break from school, there's really no reason to continue on a school schedule."

"I can't object to that," replied Madeline. "Anyone else?"

"You already know I'll never object to sleeping in," replied Jaiden.

"I have no qualms. I think I'd prefer this, actually, to account for any... 'jet lag' that may end up happening," agreed Gavin. "I'm not sure if that'll be a problem here, but it doesn't hurt to be cautious."

"Everyone else agrees, so I don't mind either," added Mishaela.

"Then that'll be the plan. No rush in getting up super early," Madeline decreed. "We will wake up comfortably, adjust, and then carry out the day's duties."

The next day, everyone rose later than the previous day, content that they could do so since they didn't have to worry about getting to school. It was always a good feeling, to not have that sense of urgency.

"I planned for us to meet with the Resistance today," Madeline told everyone as they finished eating breakfast. "We'll be leaving in about an hour, so go get ready."

It was then that everyone dispersed, to gather anything they might need for the trip, and to clean up and find some clothes.

"I was not expecting this place to have hot water, but thankfully, I was wrong," Jaiden said as she happily emerged from the shower, a trail of steam escaping the bathroom. Once back at her bed, she slipped on a black dress and started to try to wrap the folds of the sari she'd chosen— this one a deep emerald brocade with silver floral accents— earlier than everyone else so that the group wouldn't be held up by her... again. Of course, she could always just wear a cloak like the day before, but she'd decided she had to save her pride.

"Yeah, the water gets really hot, too!" agreed Jasiela. "It's a pleasant surprise."

"If I had to take a guess as to why, maybe that's because it's so sandy and dusty here?" guessed Mishaela. "Things probably get really grimy here, under those conditions. We weren't even out for long yesterday, and my glasses got all icky."

"Yeah, so did my hair..." agreed Jasiela. "I tried to put it up so I could avoid that, but I left some of it out accidentally."

"Are we ready?" asked Madeline from the front door. She'd gotten dressed before anyone else had even gotten up for the day.

"Sure, Mom," Jasiela replied jokingly. "Has anyone checked on Gavin, by the way?"

"There's no need."

Gavin emerged from his bedroom, wearing a set of a buttoned shirt and loose parachute pants, both made of a beautiful navy blue silk. "These clothes are nice. Really comfortable. So, we're going now, then?"

"Yeah, let's get going," agreed Madeline.

As everyone walked, Jasiela asked, "What kind of people are in the Resistance, anyway? Are they the plucky justice types you read about in books and stuff, or are they kinda world-weary? Or somewhere in-between, maybe."

"I don't know," replied Madeline. "I haven't yet met them in person. The only communication I had was with their, uh... executive planner? I think that was their title, if I remember correctly, who sent a message by dove regarding a meeting place and time yesterday before you all came. Someone called 'Phoenix,' so I guess there's a good chance they don't use their real names."

"Very rebel-like, I gotta say." Jaiden clearly approved.

"I suppose this is a rather redundant question, but where exactly are we going?" asked Gavin. "I'm only asking because I don't see any buildings as of yet."

Madeline took a few moments to check and be sure they were alone before answering this question.

"The Resistance has established its headquarters adjacent to the local river, as I may have previously mentioned, in a modest, unremarkable building. Through my communications with Phoenix, they've given me enough details to be able to locate the place; as far as I know, the reason we can't see it just yet is because it's a really small building. Once we get closer to the river, it'll be visible."

"Ah, I understand," Gavin nodded. "Thank you."

"So, another question that probably goes to Madeline. Once we find the place, how do we get in?" asked Jaiden. "I can only assume that if it's a resistance faction, they take the steps to make sure you can't just walk in. That'd be how they keep themselves from being discovered by the authorities, right?"

"Right. Don't worry about that, I was given instructions on how to progress past that too," replied Madeline. "As a matter of fact, look. There's the building, over there."

The destination: a brick fixture of a sandy brown color with a flat tin roof, which from this distance didn't appear to be too much larger than a tool shed. The field between the five and the building looked to be rather unassuming— just an expanse of yellowing grass that reached one's shins— but when Mishaela moved as though she was going to continue walking, Madeline put an arm out to stop her.

"Don't move!" she said hastily.

"I-I was just gonna scratch my nose," Mishaela said softly, but now sounding a lot more nervous than she was two minutes ago.

"Sorry. It's just, it's better if I show you."

Hesitating a moment to think, Madeline then pulled a pin out of her hair and threw it forward, into the grass. Within seconds, multiple thin bolts of electricity struck it, and it had evaporated into tendrils of black smoke; the pulse of the charge had been strong enough that all five of the group had faintly felt a bit of a shock within their shoes.

Mishaela cradled her arm a bit closer to herself, then.

"Holy hell," Jaiden said softly.

"I think you get the point, but just in case: stay with me, guys," Madeline said then. "There's a very specific path that's safe, and that's the one we'll need to adhere to in order to get into the building without being toasted. Now, follow me."

And so, like obedient little ducks in a row, Madeline's younger companions fell in line behind her.

When the group arrived near the building, they realized that it was at least triple the size it had seemed to be before they had traversed the invisible maze. It didn't appear to have many windows, and the sandy color of the bricks used to make up its interior were a similar color to the dry grass surrounding the area, so there was some level of camouflage going on. It made sense.

A tall man wearing clothes of the darkest blue was standing outside of what seemed to be the building's only door. His attire concealed most of his body, but from what could be seen, he had a somewhat muscular build, and skin the shade of raw umber. There was also some hair poking through his head wrap, black and a tiny bit of gray; based on the manner in which it protruded, the rest of it seemed to be pulled back into a ponytail. Although he had already seen the group when they had made it about halfway through the maze, he made sure to not turn his watchful eye to them until Madeline had stepped onto the stoop with him.

"You must be the ones that Laelia summoned," he said, a hint of happiness in his deep voice.

"What makes you say that..?" Jaiden asked.

"I have the emblem, and so does he," replied Madeline. "I can tell you what it is, but it'll have to wait until later, for probably obvious reasons." She then nodded, "Yes, we are, sir."

The man then nodded in reply, and took a step backward and gestured into the house, Jaiden staring at him as she passed him to try to determine what the "emblem" was. Nothing about his attire looked particularly fascinating, so it wasn't something that was easily seen.

Kind of impressive, when you think about it.

"Most of us don't use our names... but," he informed the youths as they walked down the corridor, "with that in mind, I am the leader of the Resistance; you all can call me Thunder."

Jasiela giggled. "Sorry," she apologized. "That caught me off guard."

Thunder nodded. Although he was a tall, somewhat stocky man, he gave off a friendly aura; this combined with the hint of a southern drawl in his baritone voice made him seem like someone that the group could trust.

I hope we're not mistaken in believing that, Madeline thought to herself.

"This here is our HQ, which you oughta have already guessed. Probably not as inconspicuous as it could be, what with it being the only building in the immediate area, but it doesn't really raise much suspicion because of how it looks on the outside. And that's what we had been goin' for this whole time: modest and unassuming on the outside, but havin' everything we need on the inside. Y'all follow me down this corridor here, and we'll be heading into the room at the very end of the hall."

The hall which everyone was now walking down had its walls and even its ceiling painted an iridescent dark blue, so that when any light reflected off of it, it cast an electric blue hue. The walls were bare, as to be expected from a place that existed out of a certain level of necessity. There were doors, periodically, made of oak, but in the direction they were going, there wasn't one; instead, the hall opened up into a bigger area, about the size of a living room.

Everyone was led to a surprisingly elaborate meeting room; many chairs with maroon cushions sat around an elongated round table, which had a map of the village unfurled on it. Thunder then gestured toward two other rebels in this room, one huge male easily over six feet tall and either very muscular or very fat, and one female who was about average height, and looked to be on the chubbier side; it was difficult to tell because they, too, were covered in the type of clothing that Thunder wore. "This is Tornado, and that's Phoenix," he introduced them. "Their roles in the Resistance are the most vital to this operation, so they'll be assisting us with forming a plan. Tornado, Phoenix: these are the five we've been discussing, the ones who will lead the rebellion." He gestured to the teens. "Why don't ya introduce yourselves? Since you aren't rebels, your real names will be fine if you want."

Jaiden was the one to step forward to introduce everyone. "Good afternoon," she said. "I'm Jaiden Winchester. This is Madeline Navarro, Mishaela Pagliardi, Jasiela Alfaro, and Gavin Harplein. It's an honor."

"It's a pleasure to meet you," the woman, Phoenix, spoke. "If only it were under better circumstances."

"They're awfully young," Tornado said, staring particularly at Jasiela. She was noticeably shorter than the rest of the group, who were otherwise all very close in height.

"Reckon that's true. But as we all should know by now, the size of a rebel doesn't determine their spirit." Thunder held a hand out toward the chairs. "Pleasure to have y'all here. Please, sit. We have pressing matters to discuss."

Everyone sat, and the teens helped themselves to the appetizers that had been sitting on the table. It wasn't much, just an assortment of round crackers with a slice of some kind of white cheese and either a grape, apple, or some other berry on top. They served their purpose, though; the ones with apples on top seemed to be the most popular based on how many were left.

"Oh. It would seem that the village isn't very big," Jaiden said, as she studied the map. "Take a look, guys. I think that's our place right there on the west end, and the plaza where the market we went to is, is over here on the east end. We're currently somewhere around here, where the river cuts off the village at the south, and the dictator's palace is at the north."

"So, when we went to the market, we pretty much walked the entire east-to-west range of the village," Mishaela mumbled. "Interesting."

"And it seems as though the palace isn't modest at all," added Gavin. "It takes up quite a bit of space on the map."

"We saw it when we went to the market last night," Jasiela told him. "Modest is the *last* word I'd use to describe that place. Whoever that dictator guy is, he either has a flair for the dramatic and intimidating, or he's compensating for something."

"What is the dictator's name, anyway?" asked Madeline. "I've been wondering that."

"The Dictator," Phoenix said.

"Yeah, him. What's he called?" Madeline reached down to scratch her foot.

"No, he's called The Dictator," Phoenix told her. "You see, around when he first came into power, he's quoted as saying, 'my name is unimportant, compared to the fact that I shall dictate.' Since then, it's stuck. He even refers to himself as The Dictator."

"Well, *that's* awfully original," Gavin said sarcastically.

Jaiden laughed.

"In fact, there are tales of people being severely punished for using his given name back when he first came into power," added Phoenix. "These days, attempting to uncover what that name is, is also punishable."

"Yikes." Madeline frowned. "That is awfully… specific."

"Trust me, we think it's just as ridiculous as it sounds to you," Phoenix agreed, a subtle chuckle at the end of her sentence. "I'm sure people wouldn't mind not using his birth name if he just said that, but the legislation and overall dramatism around it all is exhausting, so no one really bothers anymore and goes along with the whole The Dictator thing."

"Guess it's kinda like when your parents keep bothering you to do the dishes, so you do it to shut them up," Jasiela said then, making all the other teenagers nod in agreement, with a few words of assent.

"So, why don't we start our plan now?" asked Jaiden.

"An excellent idea," agreed Thunder. "Allow us to share some of our knowledge with you about the town and its environs."

The rebels proceeded to explain places where everyone could hide things, routes they could use, secret passages into the castle, et cetera, that could be considered when formulating a concrete plan. "Wait, what would we need to hide?" Jasiela asked, obviously confused by the concept.

"Reinforcements," Thunder replied. He looked at all of the youths and, upon realization that they weren't children and he didn't have to euphonize he rephrased it, "Ammunition."

At the very mention of the word, Mishaela's face went pale. "You didn't say people would have to die."

The table went silent then, in an uncomfortable way.

"Well... we'd prefer it if that weren't the case, yeah." Thunder nodded. "Actually, we've been doin' our damndest to try and make sure it's *not*, which is partly why it's taken so long to start moving forward on a plan at all. The problem is that, no matter which way we try and spin it... ya see..."

Tornado added condescendingly, "It's a revolution. People are *going* to die, sweetie."

Mishaela stood up, and bravely stood in front of the huge rebel. "I'm not your sweetie," she said. "My name is Mishaela, and I would thank you to address me as such." She sat down again, shifting back to her usual calm mood.

Madeline and Jaiden, the two people who knew her, were shocked.

"You're oddly antagonistic today," Phoenix said then, turning to Tornado. "It doesn't seem smart to alienate people who are specifically here to do what we couldn't do alone."

Tornado seemed to just brush that statement off.

"Now." Mishaela crossed her legs, in a very feminine manner. "If I may have the floor for the moment, these are my current thoughts: if history has taught us anything, it's that dictators tend to be greedy and egotistical. Do these words not describe your dictator? Actually, many historical dictators have been able to be defeated *because* of their overconfidence."

"History enthusiast here, cosigning that last part," Jaiden added. "I could give you a bunch of examples, but in the interest of time and all, I'll just leave it at that."

"Why not use that to our advantage, then?" suggested Mishaela.

"You may be on to something." Thunder nodded. "Now, if we're gonna go that route, we need to determine how exactly we could use that to our advantage. This is where I would've been happy to give y'all some sort of intel about specific ways in which the guy is up his own ass, but truth is, he's just like that in general. You ever meet anybody that's convinced they're better than everyone at everything?"

"Oh boy, have I," replied Jasiela softly.

"Okay. In that case..." Mishaela thought. "We could always make him an offer he can't possibly refuse."

"We're going to... force entry and then talk?" Phoenix asked. "Unorthodox."

"*But* not impossible," Mishaela countered. "Is it?"

"If you go through the proper channels, it ain't hard to be granted an audience," Thunder replied. "So getting into the palace itself and facing the head honcho is actually the easier part of the whole thing. If we come up with a way to use that audience to make some type of offer... well, it sure *is* unorthodox."

"No one ever said orthodoxy was required to lead a revolution. After all, you adults are going to be led by a bunch of teenagers who barely know this village, and that's quite unorthodox as well, isn't it?" Mishaela smiled.

"I like the young'un's spunk," Thunder said then. "And as I'm sure y'all would all agree, a plan that would minimize the amount of casualties is a plan the Resistance will always consider."

"Yes, definitely agreed," replied Phoenix, nodding. She then turned to Mishaela. "It sounds like you might already have an idea of how we would go about this. Am I right?"

"I think I might. I don't think it would be a good idea to eliminate the possibility of weapons completely. Maybe... if I were to suggest securing the perimeter for our meeting, and perhaps use them as a last resort? After all, if it's just us going in, we don't want to be rendered defenseless."

"Excellent callout." Thunder nodded. "I have a few ideas on how we could prevent that. What if we started everything with a group here, to the east..."

Jaiden smiled proudly. *Mishaela is starting to sound like her sister.* Chiara studied law at school, and when she needed to talk as if to persuade people, she was damn good at it.

When she talks at all, that is.

"...and overall will be a lot safer that way too. That's basically it, but of course, I'd have to run through all of this with our combat trainer to be sure we have the competence and manpower to pull it off," Thunder finished. "He around, Phoenix?"

"I think he's busy with fishing or the chickens today," she replied. "It's probably not the best time to interrupt him. That *is* our dinner."

Thunder nodded. "Y'all don't need to wait around for that, if you don't wanna. We can take it from here."

The room was still, in silence now that Mishaela and Thunder had hammered out a basic outline of a plan.

"You know, I think I like this idea," Gavin finally said.

"I'm glad we could all reach an agreement on a basic plan of action," agreed Phoenix.

"Same here." Thunder smiled, obviously relieved at the shift of things, and handed Gavin a map. "For your quarters. Here on our end, we'll continue to hash out the specifics on securing the perimeter of the palace, and getting you an audience, so don't worry about that. Y'all just come up with how you're gonna handle that meeting once you're in there. There are notes on The Dictator at your place; use them as you see fit. We'll be in contact."

"Thank you," Madeline said, giving everyone a polite bow. The rest of the group quickly followed her example.

"I assume we'll be communicating the same way we have been, then?" she asked then.

"Yes, I'll be checking in on you regularly," replied Phoenix. "If you have any questions about operations, direct them to myself or Thunder."

"I'll do that," replied Madeline.

"Travel safely," Thunder waved as everyone left.

"You are impressive, Mishaela," Gavin complimented her when they'd successfully exited the invisible maze and were on their way back to base. "To have not only thought of all that you did in such a short amount of time, but to stand up to such a large, imposing man; I don't believe I'd have had the courage to do so."

She smiled. "Thanks," she said. "It wasn't easy. My heart was pounding inside my chest the whole time. I'm not sure where it came from, really. But I guess I have too much pride to be condescended to."

"Aw, don't be shy about it," Jaiden said, waving her hand in the air as if she was swatting a bug away. "Did you see the look on that big guy's face? He wasn't expecting it, but you straight *treated* his ass!"

Jasiela and Gavin looked confused. "Treated?" Jasiela repeated.

"It's a localism," Madeline told her. "It's the equivalent of a burn, if you will."

"*Oh.*" She nodded in understanding, and they continued the walk home. "So, there's something I don't understand. Thunder said there's info for, you know, the thing we need info for-" her eyes darted around, making sure they were alone. "Where exactly would that be? I haven't seen anything like that yet."

"I'm not sure either. But I don't think any of us have explored the entire house yet, so we should do that when we get in," suggested Madeline. "Most likely, it's all kept in a room we haven't taken the liberty of exploring yet."

"Gotcha." Jasiela nodded. "I guess we can't really talk too much about this until we get in, but it would be a good idea to think of... assigning roles to our research, or something?"

"Great idea!" Jaiden pointed a finger. "We could really play to our strengths that way! For example, I'm awful at studying, but Mishaela's really good at it, so we should probably leave all the heavy reading to her. Know what I mean?"

"Real smooth, Jaiden," Madeline said with a laugh.

"What? What did I do?"

The others didn't answer her, just continuing to walk silently.

"Hey! Guys! I'm serious! What did I do?!" Jaiden continued to ask as they continued on the way home.

Chapter Six

The Planning Phase

When the group got back to base, Madeline mounted the map Thunder had given them on the wall in the living room. Looking at it she said to Jaiden, "My first thought, when I look at this map, is that before the rebellion officially starts, we might want to get closer to the palace. There don't seem to be many exits from the marketplace, so if we're not already there, the guards could easily shut us out. Maybe meet in the square about fifteen minutes before?"

"Hm. Maybe," she replied, tapping her chin with her index finger. "The combat trainer guy they mentioned may have already thought of that, though."

Meanwhile, Gavin was in charge of reading the one book on The Dictator that was easily findable in the house, and compiling notes. He looked busy, so Jasiela sat in front of him and asked, "Anything so far?"

Gavin pushed his wavy brown hair behind his ear. "Nothing surprising," he said. "From what I've read so far, Mishaela's hypothesis was correct; our antagonist is in fact egotistical. According to this book, he has multiple statues of himself throughout his palace. Not only that, but it's also stated that he has three servants whose specific job is to hold a mirror up for him for ten minutes while he gazes into it."

"Ew," Jaiden said. "I don't care who you are, no one should be *that* in love with themselves."

Gavin kind of laughed, as he continued telling everyone the results of his search so far. "In line with what we heard at the Resistance HQ, it still seems that the man's origins are shrouded in mystery. There's not really anything about what his life was like before coming to this region, other than some theorizing about where he may have come from... but of course it's difficult, impossible even, to tell what any of it means because we aren't familiar with the regions of this place. As for information that's more interesting: I found, also, that he's an impulsive gambler; it's how he was able to afford the means to take over the..." His eyes widened, darting back to the book. "'The Dictator prides himself on being the most skilled player of a particular game of which he created five years ago—'"

Jaiden then sat on the floor with the two. "This sounds like an opening to me!" she said. "Ego meets gambling."

"Yeah, precisely," Gavin agreed, nodding, before returning to the book. "'The Dictator has been known to hold audiences to just about anyone for the purpose of playing the game, so that his subjects may experience the humbling feeling of losing the game to him. The bets are often extremely high. There are some unconfirmed stories that he's even bet his palace before.' Wow, this bloke has a problem."

Gavin scanned a few pages silently after that, until his face dropped completely.

"What, what gives?" Jasiela asked.

"This book doesn't give any word as to what the game actually *is*," replied Gavin. "Without that piece of information, it'll be difficult to capitalize on this as part of our plan... unless you all have any ideas?"

Jasiela shook her head. "You got me," she said.

"Aw, man," Jaiden said, snapping her fingers. "And we were so close."

At this moment, Mishaela walked into the room, eating a skewer of crunchy shrimp. "Why the long faces?" she asked, offering the plate.

Jaiden took a skewer. "It sounds like we have a real shot at beating this guy," she said. "But it all lies upon playing a game that wasn't named in the one reference we have, so we have no idea how to use that to our advantage."

She then took another skewer, and Mishaela grabbed her hand. "Wait a second! I think I know where we can research that!"

"Really?!" Jaiden asked excitedly.

Everyone turned toward her, their dismayed faces turning into smiles.

"You're a lifesaver, girl!" Jasiela said.

"Let's not forget one thing, before we get too carried away," Madeline said as she walked over to the congregation on the floor. "The game we have to play against The Dictator most likely isn't a regular game. If the stakes are as high as they say in Gavin's book, it's honestly probably one of the most difficult games to exist, and definitely not anything we're used to considering its origin."

"Oh, yeah," Jasiela said. "The book did say it was created by The Dictator, 'member?"

"And if he created it, there's a good chance that nothing like it exists back home." Mishaela looked down at the floor, dejectedly, but almost instantly perked up. "When I said I knew where we could research this, I discovered while I was cooking that there's a gigantic library in this building; I was looking over the floor plans when I noticed it. It's probably the best place to begin looking for more information about things specific to this area, so why don't we check it out?"

"That's a good idea," Jasiela said, snapping her fingers. "Let's check it out. Where is it?"

"It should be in the basement," Mishaela informed everyone. "We can get there via a staircase in the dining room, but it's kind of hidden behind that case of knickknacks. A very clever design choice, I'll have to admit."

Jaiden hopped to her feet, pointing toward the dining room dramatically. "Onward!"

"You're such a dork." Madeline laughed as she walked past her, shaking her head.

The entire basement was, predictably, the library. The whole place was decorated in a very medieval way: stained glass windows, huge bookcases with ladders aplenty to reach the higher shelves, stone walls— that sort of thing. There were even a few (obviously expensive) chandeliers. Everyone stood for a moment to take it all in.

"This kind of reminds me of the library at school, except much more large and impressive," noted Mishaela.

"It's magnificent," Madeline said breathily.

"It's *huge*," Jaiden added. "It's going to take forever to find anything we're looking for!"

"Why don't we split up?" Madeline suggested. "Obviously, we'll cover more ground that way, and if anyone finds something interesting, give a holler."

The idea was met with no dissent, so with that, the group dispersed in five directions.

Once she'd decided on a starting place, Jaiden spent about ten minutes looking through the books at eye level before realizing they weren't even alphabetized, or categorized. "Great," she complained. "This is gonna take a long time at this rate."

She sat on the floor then, and looked at the books on the lowest shelf.

"Who even put these here?" she wondered aloud. "They look *ancient*."

She picked up one of the books, titled "Village Pastimes," and sat in a nearby wooden chair as she began to read. Sadly, the book was written at a fifth-grade level; she went through it in less than a half-hour because of it. It didn't even so much as hint at whether or not any of the games were the one that had been created by the Dictator.

Strangely... it actually didn't mention The Dictator, either.

Jaiden decided, upon realizing this, that something was off about that book. After some speculation as to why, she remembered that The Dictator had, at some point, ordered that a picture of himself be printed in the front inside cover of every book that had been published in his reign; something like a certification. That was how she already knew how he looked: tanned skin, dark curly hair, a really long, pointy nose, and shifty eyes; she was getting tired of looking at his face. She put the book back on its shelf, and picked up another that had been sitting by the first one. This one had pictures. Pictures of a happy, thriving community. And once again, no endorsement picture.

The pictures in this book were obviously not the place— or, rather, the *time* (she thought as she suddenly got an idea)— she was in.

She then climbed the ladder to the top shelf and grabbed a book. This one was in better condition, but still showed no mention of The Dictator, and no picture.

What if the books are sorted chronologically?

"Anyone around here?" she called out.

"Yeah. It's Jasiela. I'll come over there." Her feet pattered against the floor as she walked.

When she made it over, Jaiden climbed down the ladder. Once Jasiela reached the bottom, Jaiden leapt off the last rung, turning to face her. "I think I found something out," she told her. "The books are more than likely sorted by time."

"Oh..." Jasiela said, looking like she'd just had an epiphany. "When I realized they weren't in alphabetical order, I got a little thrown, but I guess that explains a lot. But, how does that help *us*?"

"Well, for starters, it means our book isn't in this area," Jaiden replied. "These are all before The Dictator came into power, because not only do they not have his stupid face plastered in them, the photos that are in them are definitely not how this village has looked in a long time— but definitely look like what it could've been decades ago. Remember what Gavin said? He mentioned when the game was created, and gave us a time and everything. But I don't remember exactly what he said..."

"Then, that means there's only one thing we can do," Jasiela said thoughtfully.

"What's that?" Jaiden asked.

"Let's go find Gavin."

"Oh. Yeah. Duh." Jaiden laughed. "I think he went this way when we all split up, let's roll."

After looking through a few of the aisles, the two found Gavin, who looked to be busy within the contemporaries, which was perfect. "Oh, hello there," he said. "Have you found anything yet?"

"Not anything tangible, but I guess that's why we're here." Jasiela folded her arms.

"Gavin, remember when you told us about the creation of the game?" Jaiden asked. "When exactly did that happen, again?"

He thought, trying to remember the exact time. "Five years ago, as I recall," he replied. "Why do you ask?"

"We need to find the books from around that era," Jaiden told him. "They're organized chronologically."

"Ah, that makes sense! The books I've sifted through thus far seemed to be building upon each other, so a chronological setup seems like it could be plausible. In that case," Gavin pointed to his left, "I noticed that the books end right over there, so I'd say those are most likely the ones that were most recently published and acquired. Let's suppose that each bookcase holds a year's worth of books. We'd have to end up right over..." He counted five bookshelves, and pointed to the one he ended on, "there."

"Excellent," Jaiden said. "Gavin, why don't you go track down Madeline and Mishaela? That way, we can all look around that area together."

"Good idea," he said, raising a finger and pointing at her. He then went to do just that.

Jaiden and Jasiela met up with the girls at their destination, and proceeded to search. Jaiden had barely started to look when she got a very strong feeling of deja vu again, the exact same feeling she'd felt when she and Mishaela had been in that flower shop, right before they'd arrived here. She intended to ask if she was the only one who felt this way, but everyone else was still searching diligently, so she assumed that she was indeed the only one who was experiencing this feeling. Turning around, this feeling led her to climb up a nearby ladder and on top of the bookcase. And so, she fearlessly climbed the ladder and discovered an extremely dusty book sitting at the very top of this particular bookcase.

"What's this?" she asked herself, picking it up. The amount of dust made her cough a little, but nevertheless, she brought it down for the others.

"Look what I found!" she said sing-songily, and gave the book to Madeline.

"Hm?" She blew the dust off of the cover. "This is... 'The Know-Hows and Go-In-Betweens of Flustered Chess, The Official Royal Game,'" she read. "Ha! This is it! The title is a dead giveaway!"

"Great job finding it, Jaiden!" added Mishaela.

Everyone crowded in to give her a group hug. When they had released her, Gavin looked up at the shelf. "How *did* you know to look up there for the book, Jaiden?" he asked, looking confused.

She smiled at him. "Call it a hunch," she replied elusively. "But that's not important right now. We have a job to do. I believe this is for you," she handed the book to Mishaela.

"Yes, thanks." She grabbed it and instantly the dust made her sneeze. When she had composed herself, she said, "Wait. Why is this for me, again..?"

"Pretty sure you're the only person here who would know how to play any type of chess," replied Jaiden. "Feel free to jump in here if I'm wrong, guys."

No one made any moves to correct her. "I mean, I know some of the rules of a regular game of chess, but..." Madeline trailed off. "Mishaela knows the rules well enough to actually play a game, so that puts her way ahead of me."

"So there you go," Jaiden gestured toward the book with both hands.

"I see. You know, for the game to have been invented just five years ago, there's an awful lot of dust on this book. It's really strange," Mishaela said as she flipped through the pages.

"Yeah, you're right," Madeline agreed. "And the placement of it— it's like no one wanted us to find it." She exhaled deeply. "Conspiracies aside, we can worry about that later, though. For now, I believe we have a date with a chessboard."

"From what I've skimmed in this book just now, yes," replied Mishaela. "Let's go back upstairs. There'll be more room for me to study this, and for you all to observe me doing so."

"Good thinking," agreed Madeline. "And we can also study these other books I found~!"

"Oh, dear..." Jaiden sighed. While not as studious as Mishaela, if a certain subject caught Madeline's interest, she would study it intensely. That was what she'd been doing with aliens and the supernatural for at *least* a decade, and was why it was easy for her to spend hours talking about that exact subject. Thinking about it now, it was almost a miracle that she hadn't immediately latched onto and started theorizing about the magic theory regarding how they were all here now.

"Don't you 'oh dear' me, these could be useful to us in the long run," Madeline said, sounding a bit offended. "They're books about the history and culture of the village we're in now, and I'm hoping it'll help with understanding this place better. It might even be a good idea to share these with the Resistance, just in case they don't know some of the stuff we find in these."

"Why wouldn't they?" asked Jaiden. "They live here."

"Just because you live somewhere doesn't mean you know everything about it; plus, no one's read every book ever," replied Madeline. "There could be some interesting nuances mentioned in one specific book, which could happen to be one that not many people are familiar with."

"All right, all right, I admit it's a good idea," Jaiden said defeatedly. "Let's get back upstairs, where we can do all this studying comfortably."

Chapter Seven

Flustered Chess

E veryone reconvened in the larger bedroom.

"This is an interesting game," Mishaela said, scarcely looking up from the book as she read. "According to this book, a game of flustered chess also incorporates some rules of checkers and marbles, and instead of eight pawns, there are only six. The other two are replaced by two unconventional pieces, a jester and a mage."

"That all went over *my* head, I can tell you that," Jasiela said, laughing a bit. "It all sounds really difficult, Mishaela; are you sure you can do it? We'll try not to be too disappointed if you can't."

She shook her head, finally looking up at all of her companions. "Although I admit that I'm not completely grasping the concept just yet myself, I think it'll be a little easier to understand once it's set up in front of me, which means I'll need a chess board. Are there any here?"

"I think I saw a couple in the parlor. I'll go get a board," Gavin volunteered.

After he'd left the room, Jaiden glanced at the book, and then a thought suddenly occurred to her, like a whisper in the wind. "Mishaela, how well can you see without your glasses, again?" she asked her.

She looked up at her, startled. "I don't know," she admitted.

That's not a sentence I'm used to hearing from Mishaela.

"It's just that I'm so used to using them, I guess I never really thought about it; and the only time I have them off is when I wake up in the morning, going to take a shower, and when I'm going to bed at night; so those times aren't exactly the best indicators of my true vision."

"Why do you ask that, Jaiden?" Madeline asked, a curious look on her face.

"I'm seriously doubtful that The Dictator will play fair," Jaiden replied. "There's gonna be some kind of bet involved, right? Doesn't that mean there's usually conditions we have to meet? Suppose that one of the stipulations to the match is that he takes away your glasses."

Everyone sat, contemplating this.

Gavin returned then, carrying a board and some very exquisite chess pieces. "What's wrong?" he asked. "What did I miss? What's got you all so sober?"

"Well," Jasiela explained, "since we're collectively doubtful that The Dictator will play fair, we were discussing the possibility of Mishaela playing this game without her glasses, except we've just learned that she doesn't know if she can even see without wearing them. Excellent situation, really."

"Ah, I see. I don't think that's cause to fret too much, though. There's an easy solution to figuring that out," Gavin said, walking over to Mishaela and holding his hand out. "Your glasses, Madame?"

"Um, okay." She took them off. "But be careful. There's a strong possibility that I absolutely need these for daily life– not to mention the cost of getting them replaced."

"Or if they even *can* be replaced here," added Jaiden.

"I promise that I will be as careful as the circumstances allow," he said, giving her a smile; one which she possibly didn't see. "Could you also close your eyes? Just a moment."

He then whispered to the rest of the group, "Move around!" After a second of confused hesitation, the three shuffled their positions so that it should be obvious they had all moved.

"Now. Mishaela, everyone else has moved to a different place in the room. Open your eyes; can you see where they are now?"

A few seconds of noiselessness made the room feel slightly more tense than it had been when everyone had been speaking.

"I'm pretty sure I can," Mishaela replied. "There's Jasiela, Madeline is over by the door, and Jaiden is right there beside the closet. I can't really see the fine details of their appearances, but I can tell who they are by their color palettes and overall shapes."

"We should be fine," Gavin concluded, as he gave Mishaela her glasses back. "But to be sure, you may want to set the chessboard up with these still off, for the extra practice."

"Right, good idea." Mishaela nodded.

She began to set the pieces on the board. Instead of the regular black and white chessboard, this one had black and sea blue squares, and it looked like all the pieces were made of porcelain. "Ah, it makes a lot more sense now that I see it..." she said.

Then, she tilted her head, in a pensive manner.

That's trademark Mishaela for "something is wrong, but I'm having a hard time putting it into words," thought Jaiden. And, indeed, she couldn't even get the question out before Mishaela answered it for her.

"Guys, is anyone else worried about the fact that I'm the only one of us who knows how to play this game? What if something happens to me?"

Jasiela furrowed her brow. "Like what?" she asked.

"I don't know!" Mishaela bunched up her hair, a confused look on her face. "As we were saying earlier, there are stipulations with bets. And there's a lot of variables in play for this one. Magic could be involved, right? Nobody knows what could happen."

"Oh, yeah. I forgot we agreed on that theory," Jasiela said.

"Hey, it's okay." Jaiden put her hand on Mishaela's shoulder in support. "If that's the case, then I guess we have no choice but to be your bodyguards."

"Yeah! Bodyguards, ready to guard your body!" agreed Madeline.

"Really?" Mishaela asked.

"Absolutely. You protect your prize hen, when you need her," replied Jaiden. "If this isn't a 'need to' type of situation, I don't know what is."

She smiled. "You guys are the best. By the way, I just now thought of something else that might also be beneficial."

Then, she turned to Gavin and smiled; timidly, this time. "Gavin, would you like for me to teach you how to play?"

He looked confused, to say the least. "But Mishaela," he said. "I don't quite understand. The most logical choice, should you choose to teach anyone, would be Madeline. She at least knows some of the rules of standard chess. I don't know *any* of them."

"Yes, but I want to teach you," Mishaela insisted. "My reasoning being, there's something to be said about the fact that you're, you know, male. Maybe, if you end up having to go in my place, The Dictator will be less inclined to screw over another male. I mean, it might not count for *much*, but we certainly shouldn't discount the possibility."

"She has a point," Madeline agreed. "Egotistical male ruler and male chauvinism usually go hand in hand. It wouldn't hurt, right?"

Gavin nodded, as he turned to Mishaela. "Not at all. In that case: teach me, for I am your humble student."

Mishaela smiled as the two sat on opposite ends of the small card table that had been brought in by Jaiden for the board. "Let's begin, then. Do you at least know your pieces?" asked Mishaela.

"Let's see," Gavin replied, looking intently at the chessboard and thinking. He pointed to the smallest piece, with a round top. "Well, there are six of these, and I remember you saying there are six pawns in the game, ergo, these must be pawns. The horse is a knight- common knowledge, right? The tallest piece must be the king, and the second tallest has to be the queen, since they're the ones of the most importance, as I recall. I'm assuming this one is the jester, because the top of it rather resembles a jester's hat. And this is the mage, because it looks like a spell cane?" He looked up.

Mishaela smiled and clapped her hands in a feverishly happy way. "That's right!" she said. "But I'm afraid you've overlooked a couple; the bishop and the rook." She pointed to both, to show which was which. "Now, each piece has its own manner in which it moves around the board. Stay with me, all right?"

At this point, Jaiden got lost; and they were still only on the traditional pieces. Deciding that she'd just get more confused if she continued to watch, she sat with Jasiela on her bed, where she was making bracelets out of yarn to pass the time. "Mind if I join in?" Jaiden asked.

"Go ahead," she said, offering the box of yarn.

"Where did you even find this?" asked Jaiden, sorting through the yarn for colors that looked appealing.

"Closet. This tote was inside of a bigger box of cloaks," explained Jasiela. "I've been making things to pass the time, since you all obviously won't need me for a little while."

"I'll go start dinner," volunteered Madeline, putting her book down and leaving the room.

Jaiden had intended to make matching bracelets for Mishaela and herself, but she didn't know how big Mishaela's wrist was (or how tight she liked her bracelets) so she decided to just make one for herself, choosing orange, black, and lavender.

Meanwhile, in Gavin and Mishaela's tutorial game of chess, Gavin had picked up a pawn or a rook, (neither girl was sure which) and tried to cross the whole board (which even they knew was against the rules). This made Mishaela laugh so hard, her face went red.

Gavin looked at her uneasily, not realizing his mistake.

"Oh, this is... this is so too much!" Mishaela was holding her stomach at this point, taking little gasps of air to try to calm herself down. "I'm sorry, Gavin. I don't mean to ridicule you or anything. That was just... let's break. I need something to drink."

She went to get a glass of water. "You okay there?" Jasiela asked Gavin. "Pride still intact?"

"That was mortifying." Gavin sighed, but then slightly smiled. "I'm learning, though!"

"You're doing better than *I* ever would," Jaiden told him matter-of-factly.

"Are you certain?" Gavin asked her. "You seem to be selling yourself a bit short."

Jaiden nodded. "I'm sure. I know my limits."

When Mishaela returned, she informed everyone that dinner would be ready soon, and that she'd pick up on the game after dinner. It was then that Gavin volunteered to go help with dinner again, insisting that he'd benefit from the change in subject.

"Can I make one too?" Mishaela then asked excitedly, pointing to the string.

"Of course," Jasiela said. "Come on over."

Mishaela eagerly climbed into the bed with the others. "I guess I can make one for my sister. Oh, or one for my mom..."

"Why not both?" asked Jasiela, handing her the string.

"But I think you should make one for your sister first," Jaiden told her. "She already wears a lot of bracelets, so I'm sure she'll love another one. Make sure to make it black, though; I'm not entirely sure that I've seen Chiara wear any other color since she started high school."

Mishaela giggled at her. "Don't be silly, Jaiden. Chiara does wear a lot of black, but her favorite color is purple. She likes all purples, but she really, really likes lavender, and her second favorite is aqua."

"Well, of course *you* know that; you're her sister," Jaiden pointed out.

"You're right. But you've learned something now, I suppose." Mishaela nodded. "What I don't understand is why she didn't color her hair purple, if that is her favorite color. The aqua suits her, but

I always assumed people went with their favorite colors when it came to changing hair colors."

"I can't say because I haven't met her, but maybe it has something to do with her skin's undertones?" asked Jasiela. "One of my best friends cut all their hair off over the summer and bleached it, and then sprinkled some kind of seafoam green in there? And when I asked them about it, I was kinda surprised by them saying they didn't necessarily like the color itself, but thought it looks really good with their face and skin."

"Ah! That makes sense!" Mishaela nodded."I don't know much about that type of thing, but Chiara probably does."

"Aren't your parents kinda strict about makeup and beauty stuff?" asked Jaiden.

Mishaela nodded. "No unnaturally colored hair or makeup until I'm fifteen. I was fortunate enough that they allowed me black eyeliner."

"Yikes. I couldn't deal." Jasiela cringed. "Be back in a second."

The door shut then, leaving just Jaiden and Mishaela.

"I didn't have the most positive opinion of Jasiela when we first met, so I'm glad I was wrong about how she is," Mishaela said when she'd left the room. "I was worried she would be a chore to deal with."

"Oh, you caught on to that too," Jaiden chuckled. "I agree with you, though. Her attitude really put me off in the beginning, too."

"I could tell." Mishaela giggled, nodding. "Well, it's one of those circumstances where I'm happy to have been wrong."

"One of the rare ones," Jaiden laughed with her. "I mean, she still has her moments, but it's bearable. We have more annoying classmates at school, right?"

"Yeah, exactly," agreed Mishaela, as they both laughed.

When dinner was ready, everyone ate in the conference room. "How is the game coming along?" Madeline asked. "Gavin, Mishaela?"

"I've already learnt the traditional pieces," Gavin replied proudly. "When we're done here, we're going to take on the two new ones."

"And tomorrow we learn the checkers and marbles rules," added Mishaela.

"Whoa, look at you!" Madeline bit into her turkey burger. For once, they weren't eating fish; the Resistance had discovered an unattended poultry farm somewhere, and Phoenix sent them a few choice cuts along with her regards. "Not even four hours, and you're already halfway there."

Gavin smiled sheepishly. "I'm not sure this necessarily counts as 'halfway...' but at the same time, I'm a simple man, I like praise. So, I thank you."

"*So*," Jaiden said then. "Madeline, you'd been reading really intently before you started dinner. Find anything interesting?"

"Yeah, actually," she nodded. "I've learned, so far, that this village we're in is called Compositora, named as such because it's believed to be the origin point in which this world was created, or rather composed, according to local mythology. It's important to note, by the way, that even though I haven't really dabbled into the mythology yet, it does mention magic quite a few times. So this *is* something that's a really prevalent belief here."

"Is that so?" asked Jaiden, smugly leaning in close. "Regretting all that pushback you gave me about the idea yet?"

"Not just yet." Madeline crossed her arms. "I want to, but I'm gonna need to read more before I make a concrete decision on *that*. I've also read a bit about what things were like here before this place became a dictatorship, and it's really interesting. It was like... controlled anarchy, is the best way I can put it? Like, there weren't really laws or positions of power, and there were certainly issues that stemmed from that, but there were also systems of punishment that were put into place if someone's wrongdoing was too severe. Merciless stuff like being guillotined in the town square."

"Whoa, pretty metal," Jaiden said then. "So in a way, knowing that, I can kind of understand how a dictator took over here. It'd be easier to overtake a place with no authority than to overthrow an existing authority."

"Ah, you know, that makes sense," agreed Gavin. "Although I wonder. This town, it seems like the type of place you'd miss if you weren't searching for it. I wonder if there were other motives besides this just being an easy area to overtake."

"Interesting. I didn't even think of that." Madelyn nodded. "Maybe the book I was reading will touch on that. I could research it tomorrow..."

Conversation died down as everyone continued to eat.

Chapter Eight

Learning The Game

"So, how goes the game?" Madeline asked, sitting beside Jaiden as she watched Mishaela and Gavin play their first game of chess the next day, after all of the rules had been covered. They were out in the courtyard, on the deck adjacent to the back of the house; while Jaiden sat in the kitchen, in front of one of the windows that allowed one to look out into the backyard from the inside.

"I feel like I could die of boredom from watching this," was her response. "Do people really get excitement from playing chess, Madeline?"

"Well, sure. It's a different kind of excitement from, say, winning a race or finding out that you were right about those damn triangles all along, but there's a certain... rush of accomplishment one feels from winning a chess game, or pulling off a really satisfying strategic move," Madeline answered. "Of course, I can't say from experience because I've never actually won a chess game and I don't know the rules well enough to make any impressive plays. But that's how it's been described to me from my friends who are chess players. It makes sense!"

"I guess." Jaiden shrugged. "Any idea what's going on here, then?"

"Sure! They're just, uh..." Madeline stared out of the window, waiting for either person to make a move on the board. Even after

Gavin had decided to move one of his knights, she still remained quiet.

"Yeah, I got nothing."

After three more minutes passed before Jaiden stood. "Sorry, can't take it anymore," she apologized, heading back toward the bedroom.

"Yeah, sure!" Madeline said, waving. "I'll, uh, I'll keep watch here in case something important-looking happens."

When Jaiden arrived back at their bedroom, she found Jasiela, drawing. "How did it go?" she asked.

"Ugh." Jaiden sat on her own bed. "They're still playing, so I can't say for sure. Even if they were done, I probably still wouldn't know. Madeline is still watching, though; she's probably more confused than when I left her at this point."

Jasiela laughed. "I bet," she agreed. "Ey, by the way. Did you notice a little *something* at dinner last night?"

"Like what?" Jaiden was intrigued. "If you mean how good it felt to finally eat a type of meat that wasn't fishy, yeah, I noticed it all right. My taste buds were in heaven!"

"Although that's true," Jasiela said, "that's not what I meant. You noticed Gavin last night, didn't you? His furtive, longing glances at Mishaela? I don't know about you, but I ship it."

"What even..? This is weird. Whatever you think you may have noticed, you're more than likely blowing it out of proportion," Jaiden told her. "That's just how he is. It's trademark Gavin."

"You're awfully confident, to be so sure that that's 'how he is.' We've literally known him for, like, two days, Jaiden. Is your denial running that strong?"

Madeline walked in then, not seeming to have heard the previous conversation. "I figured you two would be here," she said as she took a seat between them.

"Why would we be anywhere else?" Jaiden asked, in that half-joking way that only friends could use with one another. "Help us out here, Madeline. We're having a debate."

"What's it about?" she asked as she pulled up a chair.

Jasiela informed her, "I think that Gavin has a little crush on Mishaela, but Jaiden thinks that's just his personality— so she claims. What do you think?"

Madeline thought. "Well, I have to say, Gavin does seem to be a nice guy; and by that I mean one that's actually nice and isn't just saying that, or putting on a facade..."

"Ha! I win." Jaiden put her arms into the air.

"And indeed, as the person who knows Mishaela the best, I'm sure Jaiden would notice some kind of change of energy if she was intercepting any signals. But to be fair, I could also be completely wrong about all of this."

"So, *I* win," Jasiela smiled smugly.

Jaiden frowned a little. "That does *not* mean you win. On what planet? And even if it did, are we really trusting the judgment of alien girl here? What brought you in here, anyway?"

Madeline stood up. "I was thinking that, now that we seem to have a plan for the meeting, we should finally get a move on and start to organize this whole thing; we have to make sure we don't mess it up. We only have one shot, and I don't want to think about what messing that up would mean for our chances of getting home."

"Right." Jaiden replied, and the younger two nodded.

Just imagine, if not getting this right leads us to some weird time loop where we have to keep doing it over and over... or even worse, if we get it wrong and get sent to some kind of purgatory.

The thought alone sent a chill up Jaiden's spine.

"Maybe," Jaiden said then, "one of us should carry a secret weapon in case The Dictator doesn't wanna make good on the deal or tries to run away. Or both."

"Isn't that what the rebels are for?" inquired Jasiela.

"Oh, yeah. Totally forgot about that. But also, don't forget I said this. Concealed carry has proven to be very beneficial in tight situations like this."

"Still, you can't think they'll just let us into the castle without some type of search," pointed out Madeline.

"That's also a good point. But I still think it's worth it to give it a try," replied Jaiden.

Madeline just shook her head, before pointing to the map. "My understanding is that the rebels are gonna hide in the areas surrounding the palace. Don't worry; there are no guards there."

"At all?" Jasiela asked.

"When you get to the palace vicinity, the only outside guards are the pairs that guard the doors. Given the angle and height of the stairs to enter through the front, they wouldn't be able to see the bushes below. I'm told the resistance is using that to their advantage," explained Madeline.

"Well, *that* sounds like a giant security hole," replied Jasiela.

"Remember," Jaiden said to her, "we've been hearing from everybody that— despite his standing— this guy isn't exactly a super-genius. I mean, come on. He calls himself 'The Dictator.' He couldn't even come up with a cool title for himself! That in itself screams 'I have a dangerously low I.Q.,' and I think we all know that."

This made the girls crack up laughing.

As Madeline went through the entire plan to get it all down on paper (or at least most of it; for some parts, they would still have to connect with Thunder and company to finalize it) Jaiden looked out of the window at their other two comrades. She'd never noticed how serene that courtyard felt until now. Although most of the plant life in this village was yellowing (if not already dead), the decaying grass and flowers in the courtyard hadn't yet died so much that they felt *completely* desolate. It made the area feel a lot less barren and more welcoming than any of the other outdoor areas in the entire village, for this reason.

Strange that the death of plant life isn't quite so bad in this specific area. I wonder, is it because we're on the outskirts of town, and so the effects of what wiped everything out didn't quite reach? Of course, that's assuming that everything was wiped out radially, from the center of town, when that's very likely not the case.

The first person Jaiden noticed was Gavin, who was concentrating on where his pieces were; she couldn't see the board from where she was, but she assumed that was what he was staring at. He wasn't so much as moving. Meanwhile, Mishaela watched him, arbitrarily moving a white rose petal between her thumb and finger on her left hand. Jaiden noticed that there was a point where Mishaela looked at her hand, and then dropped the petal, looking a bit disgusted while frantically wiping her hand on a nearby cloth.

I wonder what happened? Mishaela isn't so prissy that the rose's color rubbing off on her fingers would get such a response of disgust.

When Gavin finally moved a piece, she shook her head, reprimanding him and pointing out a more advantageous move (again, as Jaiden assumed).

"Looks like Gavin is having a hard time." She didn't realize she was saying this out loud.

Madeline walked over to the window. "Obviously," she said. "Mishaela's quite the stickler with this game. It comes as a surprise; I didn't think someone as relaxed and kind as her could be so strict."

"Relaxed? Mishaela?" Jaiden scoffed.

"Yeah, you've got a point. But she's still usually really kind," pointed out Madeline. "Nowhere near strict, is what I mean to say."

Jaiden shrugged. "She realizes how important this is. Since we don't know how to go home yet, we might as well think of ourselves as villagers too, and before you get into how much it must suck to live here long-term, if every history class ever has taught me anything so far, it's that dictators in general suck."

"It's October, Jaiden; you guys shouldn't even be *on* dictatorships yet." Madeline thought about it before adding, "If I remember my first year correctly, you should just be progressing past the land between the two rivers."

Jaiden rolled her eyes. "Don't even remind me. Mesopotamia was a snooze-fest. Their architecture wasn't even remotely fascinating from an aesthetic standpoint. We wouldn't even be talking about it today if not for its longevity; remember, it's the oldest civilization we have a *record* of, not the oldest that *existed*. If there had been any other older and more visually pleasing ancient society—"

"Why don't we go out into the courtyard?" Jasiela suggested, abruptly changing the topic. "It's a little stuffy in here."

"Oh. Good idea," Jaiden agreed. "Hopefully, Mishaela hasn't reduced Gavin to tears."

When they arrived at the courtyard, Gavin and Mishaela were staring at each other. Intensely staring at each other. Neither of them moved, their faces expressionless, and refusing to acknowledge the arrival of their friends.

"Uh... guys?" Jaiden said.

Both turned then, at the same time. "Oh!" Mishaela exclaimed, looking just a bit embarrassed. "I'm sorry. Gavin had the idea to teach me to not show emotions when I'm playing chess."

"It's a bit difficult," added Gavin, "especially when you have someone who— I assume, based on our interactions thus far— is typically very openly emotional like Mishaela. But when people show their emotions in a strategic game, it usually doesn't end well. I'd imagine chess is included in that genre. So—" he held his hand out— "here we are."

"Oh, I see. That's not a bad idea! How did the game go?" asked Madeline.

"We reached a stalemate," Mishaela replied. "I was disappointed, but that's when Gavin came up with the idea of practicing faces."

"A stalemate is... like a tie, right?" asked Madeline. "Wow! If you can already tie with Mishaela, you must be doing *really* well!"

"Way to put our fears at ease, my guy," added Jasiela.

"Indeed." Gavin smiled at them. "I'm glad I could do that for you."

"Now, look, no pressure, friend," Madeline said, patting Mishaela's shoulder, "but we're putting every ounce of faith we have into you. We know you can do it, though."

Mishaela whimpered. "That's still an awful lot of pressure," she said shakily.

"It'll be all right," Gavin said, with an intense amount of passion in his words. "We'll be there with you every step of the way. Well, except the actual game. You do that on your own, but... we'll do everything within our means to make sure the game goes as fairly as possible. And the more fair the game is, the more easily you'll win."

She closed her eyes and nodded, still looking unsure of herself.

"Come *on*, you've got this!" Jasiela said. "Do you really think you'll lose to some jerk who doesn't even have a real name?"

"I guess not," Mishaela said with a little laugh.

This made everyone else laugh, too. "So, anyway, I'm starved," Gavin said eagerly. "Have you finished dinner yet, Madeline?"

"I have. Follow me, youngsters, and let's feast." She walked toward the door, beckoning them to follow.

Everyone went inside then to eat dinner. "So," Madeline said, "we have to meet with the Resistance to continue to finalize the plan, to make sure it melds well with their plans. I don't think we all have to go, though. Is there anyone that doesn't want to?"

"Why can't they come here?" Jaiden whined. "I hate walking around here. There are no sidewalks."

"I think there's a reason for that," Gavin said, clearly amused by the very specific issue Jaiden had raised. "Having footpaths in town would imply we need to stay out of the way of cars. I don't believe I've seen any in the entire duration of my stay here."

Jasiela thought. "No modern cars for sure, but I think I may have seen a wagon when we visited the Resistance. Or did I imagine that?"

"Oh, yeah," Gavin agreed. "I think I saw that too. It was like a delivery wagon though, innit? I don't think people would use them for personal reasons or entertainment or anything like that."

"Hm. Got a point, I guess," agreed Jasiela.

They let the matter drop then.

"Hey, guys?" Madeline asked. "What do you think is gonna happen? You know, when we're done here?"

The area became silent as the group pondered this inquiry.

"I'd hope we get to go home," Gavin was the first to answer. "Although this has been a time, ultimately, we *were* brought here against our wills. It would be nice to resume our regular lives."

"That's gonna be a whole thing, I bet," Madeline said then. "We've been here at least a week, so you can probably imagine the type of hysteria going on within our families and people we see every day. I mean, I've already debriefed my parents and my sisters about what may happen to me if I get a little too close to proving alien existence... but I also didn't leave them any of the signals that I said I would in those briefings, so they're probably worried as hell right now."

"Ugh, I didn't think of that before," Jaiden sighed. "My poor mom and dad. I know I'm a little shit toward them most of the time, because I always thought they deserved it; but... Dad's trip is probably ruined. Mom's probably pulling out her hair from the stress. They *don't* deserve all of *that*."

"What's your take on this, Mishaela?" Gavin asked.

"I do worry about my parents, but I worry about my sister even more. She's already anxious as it is," Mishaela spoke up. "If I am to contemplate what will happen after the resolution of the chess game, then: either we all go home and pick up where we left off, or we get stuck here forever."

Jasiela sighed this time. "Now, don't get me wrong. Being stuck here would be wack. No internet, horrible food variety, it's hot as hell and all dusty outside... and that's all before you get to the whole dictator issue. But at the same time, I find myself thinking: would it be the worst thing that could happen? There are worse things that could happen than being stuck here, right? Even though my place back home is chaotic and frenzied and... loud, I miss my family, you know? But when I go back, I don't know if I'll ever see you guys again, and the past few days have been sorta fun, you know? There's worse people I could have been forced to work with. I guess."

Gavin could tell how emotional she was about to get, so he gave her a hug, and Madeline patted her hand in an attempt to comfort her.

"Not only that, would we ever be able to hear from the Resistance again?" Mishaela asked. "They've all— er, most of them have been kind to us, and that's enough for me to want them to do well once we're gone."

"Plus, I'd be really pissed if things didn't get better after all the effort we're putting into this whole excursion," added Jaiden.

"We've all gotten close in this short time, haven't we? Even so, you guys need to go back to your real families," Madeline said. "We all do. In addition to the fact that they're probably all super worried about us, we don't want to set off some kind of butterfly effect by disappearing from our world forever. Once we get everything sorted, we can find a way to keep in touch, but let's fry the big fish first."

"She's right," Jasiela agreed reluctantly.

"Yeah," agreed Mishaela. "Don't forget, back home we all have that wonderful thing called the Internet. It'll make communication as easy as pie. Or it should, at least."

They ate silently after that, probably thinking about how much they missed the Internet.

"So we'll be meeting with the Resistance tomorrow at noon, then," Madeline recapped. "I'm looking forward to it. Maybe they can teach us a little more about this place while we're there."

"You know, I didn't think about that before, and now I take back my complaining," Jaiden sat up. "Maybe, if things allow, I can get a front-row seat to watch an official revolution strategy be formed."

"And you love things like war strategies!" agreed Mishaela. "Even though we're trying our best to avoid anyone getting hurt, I can't imagine this type of strategizing being too much different than that. There's just an, er, noticeable lack of weaponry."

"*Obvious* weaponry," added Jasiela. "Remember, when we first talked to our Resistance comrades, one of them mentioned securing the perimeter? Although using them would most likely be a last resort, the people securing that perimeter will most likely have some type of weapon. That, or be armed with a moderate level of martial arts abilities."

"How do you know this?" asked Gavin.

"Spy movies." Jasiela shrugged.

"It *does* make sense, though," pointed out Madeline. "I didn't see any weaponry at the base when we went— and trust me,

I checked— so they're probably already really good at hiding weapons."

"You guys have got me all excited again!" exclaimed Jaiden, grinning. "I'll have no problem getting up tomorrow— I guarantee that!"

Chapter Nine

Revolutionary Strategy

"What happened to waking up on time, Jaiden?" Jasiela teased her as the group walked toward the Resistance outpost the next day.

"Shut!" Jaiden pointed a finger at her. "I was just having a really good dream. Yeah, that's it. Such a good dream that I couldn't bring myself to end it! So I ended up sleeping longer than I'd planned. That's all."

"You *could* just admit that you overslept." Madeline laughed.

"And you know that I would. *If* that was actually what had happened." Jaiden shrugged.

"Well, you know, regardless of reason, you *did* sleep later than intended. So, if we're using the literal definition of the word, then yes, you did oversleep–" started Mishaela.

"You guys!" Jaiden complained. "We're all here, happy and healthy, and everything is going as planned. Isn't that what's important? Now, let's– holy crap."

The group had arrived at the Resistance outpost, and the small group of people stationed just behind it, by the river, came as a bit of a shock. That was most likely because there had been a grand total of three people there for the last visit, though.

"At my core, I knew that a resistance faction had to be made up of more than three people, but actually seeing more people here is a little surprising," Mishaela said then.

"Yeah, my thoughts exactly," agreed Madeline.

"Oh, you've arrived."

Five faces turned to see a familiar feminine shape in front of the doorway. "Oh, Phoenix!" Madeline waved, noticing the outfit she was wearing was almost identical to what she'd worn last time, except it was emerald green this time. Jewel tones seemed to be popular here. "Nice to see you again."

"Thank you, same to you. So I hear you're here to calibrate your plans with ours?"

"That would be exactly why we're here!" Madeline replied. "But I'm sure we need to go inside. Best to be away from any potential prying eyes, I assume."

"You assume correctly. Follow me, and we can all confer."

Everyone fell in line behind Phoenix then, walking into the outpost building. "So, if you don't mind me asking, what's with all the guys that are out back?" asked Jaiden.

"Out back? Oh, they'll be the ones securing the perimeter of the palace for you all, so they've been running through some maneuvers for the big day. Would you like to see them practice?"

"Um. Is that even a question? Hell yes!" Jaiden nodded eagerly. "I'd love to see if they're using any historical warfare models of self-defense!"

"Even for those of us who aren't complete nerds about that type of thing, I think that just seeing what they're up to would make us all feel more confident about everything," added Jasiela.

"Okay." Phoenix gestured toward a pair of sliding glass doors, which gave a panoramic view of the group of people outside honing their skills, a reasonable distance away. "They're right out here. I can almost guarantee, though, that these guys aren't using— how did you put it, again— 'historical warfare models of self-defense.' In fact, our combat trainer kind of prides himself on his modernism."

"Well, *that's* no fun," complained Jaiden.

Phoenix slid one of the doors open and called out, using a word that sounded foreign to all the teens' ears, holding up her right hand. This caught the attention of the person leading combat practice: a rather tall, thin young man with fair skin, his dark hair waist-length and tied into a low ponytail. He wore a pair of blue silk parachute pants, and no shirt; although not muscular, his body was clearly toned, as one would expect a combatant to be.

After excusing himself from his combat group, the man walked over to the building, and as he drew closer it became clear why he was so modern in his approaches. He didn't look too much older than any of the five guests.

"Morning," he gave a salute. Looking at Phoenix, he asked with a touch of confusion, "New recruits?"

"...Not exactly..."

"Oh. *Oh*! These must be our special friends!" He grinned, eagerly going to shake everyone's hands. "It's a pleasure to be working with you all! It's so nice to meet people from the other world. I'm Logan, the Resistance's combat extraordinaire."

"Nice to meet you, Lo—" Madeline frowned, doing a double-take. "Logan..? Is that your real name?"

Logan laughed. "Yes. You see, that is an added perk of never being permitted to leave the outpost. I don't need a code name!"

"Really? Why aren't you allowed to leave?" asked Gavin.

"I'm sure your guide can explain that easily."

When Logan glared at Phoenix, she explained, "You see, Logan is my little brother."

"Little?" Jasiela was, of course, referring to how Logan was a head taller than Phoenix.

"Fine. *Younger* brother. The shortest version that I can give is: I promised our parents that I wouldn't let him come to any serious harm," explained Phoenix. "This was the most effective way we came up with for us to make good on that promise."

"My joining the Resistance was against our parents' wishes, but I also think they both knew that no matter what, I was going to follow in my sister's footsteps," explained Logan. "I kinda... showed up here without any word about it, so she wasn't too happy that I came here to join, putting myself in danger, either— so that's another reason we reached this compromise."

"Logan, if you aren't too busy, why don't you show our charges around for a minute or two?" suggested Phoenix. "I have to go locate Thunder so we can talk about our plans."

"Yeah, sure!" Logan waved. "Come on, guys. I'll show you the outpost! By the way, I don't believe I got your names. Sorry about that!"

"No problem! I'm Madeline. These are Jaiden, Mishaela, Jasiela, and Gavin. All five unsuspecting teens that probably shouldn't be wrapped up in all this, to be honest."

"Don't sell yourself too short! I myself was only fifteen when I joined the Resistance," Logan said as they walked. "Joined on paper, anyway. But no one here, including our boss, thought it would be wise to have me actively fighting the power at such a young age, so outside of small base operational duties, I was left to study until I graduated high school. That's how I ended up learning so much about combat, and obtaining my current position within the Resistance."

Mishaela noticed Logan called it "high school," trying her best to make some more sense of the environment and culture here. Logan, though, spoke noticeably differently than everyone here except Phoenix (obviously). It wasn't necessarily an accent— although he seemed to have tiny remnants of that too— but his natural cadence of speaking vastly differed from the other adults' here.

"Follow me; there's a flight of stairs in the living room. You've probably already seen the planning room, so with that being the case, there's not much more to see above ground," he said then.

"So the rest is under—" Mishaela stopped, and sighed. "I hate that that's a pun."

"A completely unintentional one, but I love it!" Logan laughed. "It's a safety precaution first and foremost, but I, personally, love the fact that this underground resistance faction is... underground."

Reaching the first basement floor, leaving everyone in a small dirt-colored room with no adornments or furniture and a door on either wall, Logan turned toward everyone, his ponytail swishing around his waist with the motion. "This is the main area on this floor. It's nothing fancy; the cafeteria is over on the left and sleeping quarters are on the right. Not all of the Resistance lives in this building, for probably obvious reasons; mostly just those of us with a title, or that don't have families on the outside. There's a staircase in the quarters leading farther down that puts us in the library."

"Oh, the house we've been staying in has a library underground too," remembered Jasiela. "Is that a thing here?"

"Correct. One can assume that all Resistance-affiliated buildings have a secret library," replied Logan. "A few of us here are dedicated to finding books and putting them away for safekeeping; this is one of the tasks I assisted with as a youngster, actually. The Resistance strives to keep our country's history and literature safe, and that's not always been a guarantee under our, uh, current management. Heck, even the books I used while I was in high school were *very* obviously modified."

"While that makes sense given the situation, it's still really sad," Jaiden sighed. "As the saying goes, those who fail to know history are doomed to repeat it."

"I couldn't agree more," Logan nodded firmly. "Now, as much as I would like to show you all my favorite books in the library, we should probably head back up; it shouldn't take *that* long to find Thunder."

When they started back, Gavin asked, "Will you be securing the perimeter with everyone else, Logan?"

"If only. As it stands, I've been delegated to stay back here," he replied. "My sister fears the possibility of a military attack in retaliation to the uprising, and she wants me here in case anything happens to her or Thunder."

"You'd take over?" asked Jaiden. "That's a lot of pressure on someone so young."

"Yeah, but that's the kind of thing you sign up for when you join a resistance," replied Logan, shrugging. "Besides, it's not like I'm a kid or anything! I'm totally capable!"

Everyone laughed. Despite only knowing Logan for about a half-hour now, he definitely didn't give off the leader vibe.

"Hey, what's so funny?!" he asked, pouting.

Madeline tried to explain, "Probably the fact that you're less a leader and more of a... a..."

"Little brother type."

Everyone turned to see Thunder and Phoenix behind them, both looking amused at the teens quickly catching on to Logan not really being leader material. Not just yet, anyway.

"If you guys really think that, then why are you leaving duties to me should you not come back?" asked Logan, obviously confused.

"Well." Thunder patted Logan's shoulder as he passed by him. "Guess that means we have no choice but to both come back in one piece then."

He gave Logan a smile then, as if to reassure him that that would be the case; that everyone would indeed come back unharmed. Logan gave him a nod of understanding, in response.

"This way, everyone, let's start our meeting." Thunder pointed down the hall, toward the planning room.

"Where's Tornado been?" asked Logan, as everyone began to walk. "I haven't seen him in a few days now that I think about it."

"He's in the planning room waiting for us," replied Thunder.

"Ah." Logan nodded. "Got it. Does he still have a stick up his ass, do you think—"

"Logan!" Phoenix scolded him, hitting him over the head (as best she could).

Jaiden just laughed to herself as Logan complained in a language she wasn't familiar with. Ah, that explained the slight accent.

And regarding Tornado— so that hadn't been her imagination— the guy really *had* had an attitude problem.

"He's had a problem ever since I've started leading combat, if not longer," Logan elaborated further. "That's way too long to be holding a grudge or anything."

"Logan." Thunder subtly gestured toward the five teenagers following them.

"Er, right." Logan nodded. "I'm sorry. Salty or not, he is a fine man that is good at his job." He said this with an intonation that indicated he didn't entirely agree with the words he was saying; almost as if he were being sarcastic.

The group made it to the room then, where indeed, Tornado was waiting, reading some book. "Everything has been set in place now," Thunder said when everyone had entered the room. "We can now begin the final stages of planning. Once everyone's settled in, we can start with Logan's strategies regarding the securing of the palace's perimeter."

"Right!" Logan had already sat down, but hopped back up to go grab a scroll. "You see, an advantage we have— which I had never even thought about until I'd started to study the maps of the region— is that..."

He unrolled the scroll on the table, covering it entirely. It was a map of the village, with various strategic markings all over it.

"The river that flows behind this outpost is the very same one that passes underneath the palace," Logan pointed to the river, using his finger to signal the direction of the water flow. "I've done multiple tests in the past to see if that passage is monitored, and I'm happy to say it isn't; so we have a couple of volunteers that are going to be able to secure the area from the inside."

"When did you find the time to do that?" asked Thunder curiously.

"Do you have any idea how boring it gets when you can't leave this place?" countered Logan. "I've done a lot of spontaneous tests and stuff to multiple ends: to absolve my boredom, learn more effective combat strategies, get a better understanding of our enemy."

"Isn't that dangerous?" asked Phoenix. "We don't completely know what the interior of the palace is like."

"Yes, I've considered that. But according to the research that I've been doing, it looks as though the area where the river passes through is almost completely unused; just a bunch of boxes there, kinda looks like a storage room," replied Logan. "So, it's actually sufficient for those infiltrating the area to just stay there. The boxes will conceal their forms. The palace's rooms aren't soundproof, and the walls are kinda thin, so it's easy to hear what's going on. Should there be a large ruckus, they'll know to go check it out.

"Aside from that, the entrance to the palace is rather close to the market, so that's another advantage."

The five teens observed, impressed, as Logan continued to explain his plan. He'd be interrupted by a question from his elders every now and then, but he was able to answer them with no difficulty at all. This came as a surprise; it wasn't at all what they were expecting from someone who had learned combat so informally, and who was still quite young. Within the hour that they had known him, he had formerly seemed a bit flighty and lackadaisical; now, it was like his personality had done a complete 180.

"And, finally, I think it would be beneficial if our special friends here were to learn at least a bit of self-defense, provided they don't have any prior knowledge," Logan was finishing his pitch. "If it fits into the overall plan, that is. It's just that I know our current reverent leader—" he said that clearly sarcastically— "isn't exactly known for fighting fair. None of us know the extent of what kind of tricks he can or will pull, so just in case physical defense is needed."

"If you need people who are good at physical combat, you'd probably be best trying to mentor Madeline and myself," Jaiden said. "She's an athlete. I simply have a lifetime's worth of skill of fighting much older brothers."

Logan laughed, but stopped immediately when Thunder gave him a look. "You are an athlete, Madeline?"

"Yeah. My parents put me in figure skating classes when I was, like, six or something, and I still do practice; just not as often as I did as a kid. These days, my practice is more strength training than anything— you know, squats, planks, curls, et cetera— so now that I think about it, I guess it *would* be a good idea to consider me for any type of physical combat needs."

Jaiden nodded. "Yeah! I mean, sure, I have some skills of my own. But I feel like what I can do is nowhere near Madeline's abilities. I'm pretty sure she could bench me, even."

Logan smiled again, clearly amused. "Very well. We can discuss it more at a later time."

"It's time for us to hear your part of the plan," Phoenix said then. "I look forward to hearing how it's coming along."

"And we look forward to telling you!" Madeline smiled happily. "Well, right after we left here, we studied using all of the tools available to us, and determined that the Dictator's Achilles heel is his overconfidence when it comes to sport. Particularly, games of chess."

"Oh!" Logan nodded. "Right. I saw a game once on my way home from school a couple of years ago. Quite the spectacle. But if you are to go this route, it is important to know that the Dictator has never lost a game."

"*Has* he not lost?" asked Gavin. "Or has he had his losses expunged from public record, and the winners disposed of somehow?"

"That's... not a bad point, actually," admitted Thunder. "Highly likely, too, when ya think about it."

"We do realize there's a lot of risk involved in this plan," added Jaiden. "But for what it's worth, I don't think I've ever seen Mishaela lose a game, either, and she's the one that'll be playing for us!"

"Well, my sister's better, but she's not here," added Mishaela softly.

"Hmm..." Thunder was thinking. "Logan, do you think you could come up with some type of signal for if your team needs to start firing?"

"Already done. Why do you ask?"

"I would imagine that the Dictator screens his opponents in some kinda way, meaning if he knows he can win against someone it'll be a public game— like the one Logan saw a couple of years ago— but, if he thinks they might be a challenge, he makes them play a private game. That way, provided we're correct about his 'solution' to his losses, they would be able to be eliminated with little to no one noticing." Thunder crossed his arms as he spoke. "But I was just now thinkin' of maybe trying to force a public game."

"How so?" asked Phoenix.

"If we cause a big enough disturbance outside the palace grounds, guards will appear. There ain't *that* many guards enlisted. If the disturbance is large enough to extract them all from where they usually post, it should draw his attention. If the game is public, I would hope he wouldn't just smite someone in midday when he's already agreed to the terms of the game; he's too proud. But even if something sneaky does happen, we'll have our guys around the perimeter."

"But what if he doesn't come outside?" asked Jaiden.

"Then we continue as we've been planning before now," replied Thunder. "Five teenagers is a pretty unsuspecting group, but if any of y'all are defense-trained, that'd come in handy."

"And we do have Gavin able to take Mishaela's place if it comes to that," added Madeline. "So there's another precaution there."

"Okay. So now, how do we cause a disturbance?" asked Phoenix.

"That's the easiest part, in a place where you can't even wear what you want," replied Jasiela. "Hey! Why don't we do that?! We could all just wear normal clothes! Maybe convince the townspeople to, too. That way, everyone in the Resistance will blend in, you know? Can't shoot everyone who's dressed normally."

"Hiding in plain sight, as they say," added Jaiden.

"Not a bad idea." Thunder nodded. "Tornado—"

He looked up. This entire time, he'd been writing; as he should, as the official recorder of the Resistance.

"Do you think you can get your guys to get the message out, and how soon?" Thunder asked.

"My team is more than capable of messenger work," he answered, if a bit arrogant. "Expect the entire village to know within the next 24 hours."

"Excellent." Thunder nodded. "I know it will take some days for all of us to be completely prepared, so if y'all could just keep in touch with us regarding strike time."

"I'll have to come visit you all as well, for some training," added Logan. "If that is that all right with you, dearest sister?"

"Don't start with me," Phoenix said, exasperated. "Of course it is. Do you all promise to shut this kid down if he starts getting too crazy with his ideas, though?"

"Will do." Madeline nodded, standing. "Thank you all so much."

"No, thank *you*," replied Phoenix. "This village has suffered for a long time, but we finally seem to be getting a chance at freedom for everyone here, thanks to your help!"

"Clearly, the goddesses have blessed us," added Logan. "Have a safe trip home, you guys."

"Yeah, see ya!" Jaiden waved, as the teens began to head out of the outpost, to start on their journey back home.

Chapter Ten

Finalization

For the rest of the day, after the five returned home, Mishaela and Gavin practiced their games of chess, with the remaining three as their audience. There wasn't much in the way of conversation while the games were going on, but it was when they decided to stop for the night that it picked up again.

"You know..." Mishaela put up a finger as she turned away from the closet, where she'd put away the chessboard that she and Gavin had been using to practice. "Something's been on my mind since earlier, when we visited the Resistance."

"Oh?" asked Madeline.

"Right before we left, Logan said something along the lines of 'the goddesses have blessed us.' In that mythology book you were reading, Madeline, didn't it say the world was created—"

"—by the magic of six goddesses. Yes, it said that," agreed Madeline. "You know, Logan behaves differently than his elders, and not just in ways that signal his youth. It's hard to explain but, like how he refers to us as their 'special friends.' And now that I think about it, since the adults of the Resistance seem to treat him like he's less of a spearhead and more of their collective little brother, they probably neglected to mention to not be too mystic around us."

"Yeah," agreed Mishaela. "You know, if we want to truly know the backstory of this place, we might get a more conclusive answer if we ask him."

"Excellent idea. He said he'll be coming over to teach us some combat stuff too, so if he comes alone, we'll have that opening," pointed out Jaiden. "Let's hope that's the case."

"Yeah, you know, when he was giving the presentation of his attack plan, he seemed really smart," Madeline said then. "I almost wonder why we weren't introduced to him earlier, but at the same time— aside from not being there the first time we visited— I could assume that it has something to do with his and Phoenix's agreement to keep him within the confines of HQ."

"As an older sibling, I understand why that was the conclusion they came to... but also, as a younger sibling, I can sense the frustration Logan has about the whole thing," Jasiela said. "It's strange, I usually don't care this much about someone I just met, but I kinda find myself hoping they give him more freedom if we pull this off. He'd deserve it."

"*When* we pull this off," Jaiden said confidently, placing a hand on Jasiela's shoulder.

"That's an awful lot of confidence. A bit cheeky." Gavin smiled, "But I like it."

"Thanks, my dude. If you believe in yourself enough, you'll have no problem inspiring others to do the same, you know?" Jaiden replied. "That's what I like to think, anyway. Now what's next? Are we going to be making any more progress on anything tonight?"

Everyone exchanged glances as they tried to decide nonverbally. "No, I think we're all just taking it easy for the night," replied Madeline. "Personally, I'll be reading in my bed until I fall asleep. See you all tomorrow!"

"I think retiring early sounds wonderful, actually," agreed Mishaela. "A lot transpired today. Rest sounds not only adequate, but almost a necessity!"

"Then let's all do that," Jaiden replied. "Night, everybody."

The next day, Logan arrived at the base almost earlier than anyone within could wake up. The sun was hardly in the sky when Madeline rolled out of bed, frustrated at the knocking on the door.

"Good morning!" Logan waved, today wearing a plain white shirt that was mostly open except for the lowest two buttons being fastened, and equally loose pants in a bright crimson red, appearing to be made of crushed velvet.

"Who the *hell* told you that showing up this early was okay? Why didn't you ask what time to come? Haven't you ever heard of courtesy?!" Madeline berated him at the door.

Logan just looked confused. "I-I, uh... I'm... sorry?"

"That is no way to speak to a superior!" Madeline was frantically pushed out of the door's view by Mishaela, who had luckily also been awakened by the knock. "Especially one that's helping us! I'm very sorry, Logan. Madeline, while usually our sensible de facto leader, has never been able to gracefully handle early rising. I hope you aren't offended."

Logan waved a hand in the air. "No, of course not. Are you kidding me? I hear worse regularly at HQ, and that's only sometimes not directed at me!"

"Oh. I see. That must be pretty rough, then?" asked Mishaela, as she stepped aside to let him in.

"Rough? I wouldn't necessarily say the situation itself is rough. It's just that, as a combat trainer, you get used to dealing with people who are... rough around the edges," explained Logan. "And that's *before* you throw them on their ass while sparring."

"I see. Does that happen a lot?" asked Mishaela curiously.

"The amount of times it happens is, honestly, a bit embarrassing," replied Logan with a laugh. "That's not to overstate my battle prowess, of course. It's just that a lot of the people that join up with us are... rugged, world-weary, usually early-to-mid-30s and pretty strong, that kind of thing. So when they tell Thunder they want to join the combat division, and are consequently told they'll be reporting to and studying under a scrawny 18-year-old like me, then, oh boy, they *lose* it. So they go into battle overconfident, not taking it seriously. I like to think of it as my job to show them why that is a grave mistake. After all, one should never underestimate their opponent, no matter what types of biases their appearance sets off in one's mind."

"Understood." Mishaela nodded. "Well, since you got here so early, you've actually gotten here before we could prepare breakfast. It would be in poor form if I didn't offer you some."

"Oh, that would be wonderful!" Logan clapped his hands together. "I'll just take whatever it is you're making for everyone else, so that I don't become a burden. I'll be waiting out in the courtyard, if that's okay?"

"Yes, that's fine." Mishaela nodded. "In that case, one of us will come get you when the food is ready— if you haven't come back inside by then."

"Good deal." Logan put a hand up, as if waving, before heading out of the door in the kitchen. Mishaela stared after him for a moment, before she went to whisk some eggs in a bowl. She had a lingering suspicion that she should follow Logan into the courtyard, but then shook off any questions she had about him for the time being and reached for the salt.

Meanwhile, in the courtyard, Logan looked around, intrigued by the fact that the grass and flowers in the area still retained some color, as opposed to plant life pretty much anywhere else in town. "Hmm..." He bent on one knee, touching the petals of one pink tulip, noticing when he rubbed his fingers together that a small amount of golden dust remained.

"Interesting. It would seem that magic hasn't completely left this place; that is a good sign."

He heard the door of the house open then, and immediately— instinctively, almost— turned to see who was joining him. "Oh. A good morning to you! Gavin, right?" he asked.

"That's right." Gavin nodded, walking down the three steps to where Logan was.

"Good. I admit, I struggle just a little more with remembering which name goes to which person for your feminine-presenting friends, but I suppose that's primarily because there are more of them," admitted Logan. "Have you come to summon me for food?"

"No, not yet. I merely wished to sit and talk for a time, if that's all right?" asked Gavin.

"Ah." Logan nodded. "Of course it is. I suppose you ask because you want to know more about our world here, right?"

"Oh. You've already found me out."

At this, Logan laughed. "It isn't an unreasonable conclusion. I'd be full of questions if I suddenly found myself in your home, so I can only conclude that it must happen the other way around as well. Ask away; although, I must inform you that my sister has sworn me to secrecy on some of the more complex details for multiple reasons, and I would like to ask that you respect that."

"Certainly," Gavin agreed, sitting on the ground where Logan had kneeled. "After all, I do believe my most burning question is: what exactly *is* this place? This building we're staying in, I mean. It must be of some significance, for it to still be safe."

"You're correct. This building actually used to be the Resistance HQ, but it was moved a mere four months before I arrived here. I know what the follow-up question to that is going to be, and I genuinely don't know the official reasons; however, I've always assumed that in addition to size constraints, it's because this became the outskirts of town after a time."

"Became?" asked Gavin.

"Ah, you noticed. Yes. There was a time where this village— in addition to being much more prosperous than it is now— was also much *larger* than it is now. In those days, this location was relatively near the middle of town. In fact, it was so that both this and the square where you'll be going to enter the palace were both considered to be within the center of town."

This revelation shocked Gavin, who remembered that these days, the distance between here and the markets was pretty much the entirety of the village. "It's shrunk that much?" he asked incredulously. "This dictator of yours really *is* that awful."

"Well..." Logan made a face, unsure of how to phrase what he was about to say next. "While I certainly cannot deny that, there are actually more factors than just him that contributed to the city's dwindling population and resources. It is a rather complicated issue; one that would require days of study to completely understand."

"Ah. Understood." Gavin nodded. "I won't pry. The other burning question I have is that, from what I do know, all of these collective things have been transpiring longer than I've been alive, if not very well longer... and so, with that being the case, I do wonder: why is it only just now that action is being taken? That's not to undermine the hard work you've likely all been putting in as the Resistance, but surely there must be something else as to why it's taken decades?"

"I wish I had a better answer, but... I do believe that's just the nature of humanity," replied Logan. "We bide our time until doom is imminent."

Gavin couldn't argue. He had already noticed this himself, in his fourteen years of life.

"I'm eighteen. This has been an issue since before even I was born, and sometimes the older guys in the Resistance get emotional when they realize some of its members don't know how life was here before all of this." Logan sighed softly. "But for me... that's part of why I work as hard as I do to aid our resistance efforts. The world that Thunder and the other elders remember this being is a world that I want my generation to know... if not a better one."

"I think that's a quite admirable goal, Logan."

"Yeah, well." Logan averted his gaze bashfully, his cheeks turning just a little red. "It's in our nature as humans to want better for ourselves and those we care about, isn't it?"

"Yeah." Gavin nodded. Maybe that was why he always got so annoyed with his brothers; if they sat still for two seconds and concentrated on something aside from intentionally creating chaos, they'd be happier… wouldn't they? Gavin liked to think so, anyway.

"Guys! Food's ready!" Madeline had opened the door to yell out to the courtyard. "Oh, and sorry for earlier, Logan."

Logan shook his head. "There's no harm done. Water under the bridge, as they say. Now, let's get to the meal so we can get to work, hm?"

After a quick breakfast, everyone followed Logan to a nice clear field just outside of town. "This is suitable," he said softly. Louder, he asked, "Does anyone have any questions before we begin? It'll be a little easier to ask without all the physical exertion."

The area became silent.

"Okay. So, do we have any volunteers, then?"

"Oh! Me!" Jaiden raised her hand. "Teach me how to kick some quality ass, Logan!"

Logan laughed. "That's what I'm here for! We can start as soon as we're done with our preliminary stretches. Give yourselves some space so we can begin."

As everyone spaced out, and began their stretches, Logan continued to speak. "Now, a disclaimer that I usually put into the warmup exercises is that— being a part of a resistance faction— there may be some circumstances you find yourself in that do not give you the ability, or the time, to warm up. In those cases, I like to be conscientious of the moves I'm using, and try to work up to the stronger ones after a few weak ones. Of course, sometimes you cannot do this either… and in that case, I can only say to try and have the appropriate remedies on hand in the event of an injury. Now, let's begin. Come at me with an attack, Jaiden."

"Wait, what was that last part?" asked Mishaela, suddenly concerned.

This was drowned out by Jaiden's following scream of effort, as she put all of her strength into a high kick— a high kick that Logan effectively (and quite easily) blocked with his arm and caught her ankle with his free hand. "I get the feeling you didn't really listen to the 'work up to the more powerful attacks' part I said, did you?"

"It wouldn't be Jaiden if she wasn't impulsive as all hell, would it?" asked Madeline, in jest.

Jaiden couldn't find it within herself to argue that, not only because it was true, but because Logan was still holding her in the kicking position and she couldn't put her leg down, and it was starting to get tired.

"I'm only still holding you in this position because I think you'll be more inclined to listen if you can't move," he explained. "Now. In situations where one cannot prepare, begin with quick attacks meant to both temporarily stun your enemy and to serve as a build-up to your larger, more powerful attacks."

"Okay, okay, got it. Can I have my leg back now?"

Logan smiled as he released Jaiden's ankle, allowing her a few moments to rest her leg before resuming his stance. "Whenever you're ready."

"Hey, Logan!" Jasiela waved her hand high above her head, to indicate that she was the one who had spoken. "So what's the consensus on us getting some sweet weapons?"

"The consensus is no. That would, unfortunately, raise a bunch of problems that none of us in the Resistance are equipped to remedy. The most pressing one, for example, would be the ability to get into the palace with a weapon. Probably not impossible, but you know. A hassle, if you were found out."

"An unnecessary one at that. We understand," replied Mishaela.

"I'm glad. Now let's continue."

Although Logan was thin, as every teenager learned as they demonstrated with him, he was definitely strong. His story of how new recruits would underestimate him made a lot of sense now; perhaps they had as well. But they all also knew that they couldn't make this mistake on the big day.

"This was a productive day. I have faith in you all. The others try to downplay it, but I know they do as well," Logan said at the end of the day. "But I would be remiss to not emphasize that you mustn't feel as though you're shouldering this all on your own. As I have faith in you, I ask that you have faith in us as well."

"Of course. Like we've been saying, we're all in this together, right?" Madeline held out a hand, and Logan shook it heartily.

"That's right. Our energies complement each other in a way that makes me feel it's safe to trust you, and so I do." Logan nodded then.

"What do you mean by that?" asked Jaiden, recognizing this as a possible way to understand Logan's cryptic mysticism.

"Ah... that is something I probably cannot get too deep into without breaking the promise of secrecy I forged with my sister, but..." Logan paused, thinking. "There's nothing wrong with a bit of a cultural lesson, I'm sure. In this world, we believe that every person has a specific type of energy that can be felt by others in their vicinity and via their interactions. And sometimes this energy is welcoming, amiable, like a friend. That is the type of energy I feel when I'm around you all; and I'm sure it's part of the reason why you were chosen for this task."

"I think I understand," Mishaela said. "I have a friend back home that speaks of similar things. But they're rooted in astrology, and I didn't once hear you mention the stars."

"The stars? Affecting one's energy? What an interesting idea." Logan looked as though he was mystified. "There's so much we could stand to learn from your society... but I suppose that must wait. Will I be seeing you all tomorrow for more practice?"

"Is the plan to do so until D-Day?" Gavin asked then.

"That sounds like a good idea." Logan waved before heading out of the door. "See you all tomorrow, then!"

And so the next few days continued this way, with each teenager practicing with Logan; consequently, learning more from him.

On the next day, Jaiden learned that Logan and Phoenix's parents were still living, and that the city the two siblings had been born in was called the City of Garnet, named as such because there was a large, tall chunk of garnet in the city center. Among recounting a few childhood memories, all seeming to paint the picture of a relatively normal environment in a small city, he had also hinted that there was some sort of cultural significance to the garnet— but quickly cut himself off when he realized how much he'd been talking.

On the following day, he told Mishaela a little more about his sister; that Phoenix had always been the type of person that wanted to help others, so it was no surprise when she began independently studying medicine, and even less of one when she left home to join the Resistance. Even though that was the case, their parents still felt the tiniest bit slighted by it and channeled that into trying to keep Logan at home— something that they probably also knew was a losing battle. But Mishaela had to wonder if Logan's parents really did want to keep him at home because they felt spurned by Phoenix, or if it was because they were genuinely worried that they'd lose both of their children, and Logan couldn't understand that.

The third day, Madeline was Logan's partner, and he spoke of how he hadn't had a lot of friends in school. He wasn't necessarily unpopular, or bullied *too* intensely, and he was even naturally extroverted and had no problem socializing and participating in events, but he was given to fading into the background due to his goals and the way he had to go about them. After all, he only lived in this town because he wanted to join the Resistance, in the first place; it wouldn't do to make friends if they may have to mourn him later. There was also the fact that, even though he usually had loads of energy stored inside, and could talk for hours about... well, pretty much anything, he was naturally quiet until something kicked off his interest. And when it didn't, he just stayed in his corner, reading and studying. This was how he gathered much of his knowledge surrounding combat and self-defense. Although he couldn't delve too deeply into the specifics, he'd also extensively studied the history and mythology of this world. He merely said that, between history and combat, he'd need at least one of them to assist the Resistance as best he could.

On the fourth day, Gavin partnered with Logan; they were mostly quiet, but now and again Logan would mention things that had begun to signify the beginning of the end, a need to rise to arms for the Resistance. There had been a bunch of small occurrences: the complete loss of color from the plants, the air quality, the waters... it was because he'd studied the history of this world that he knew that all of these things, together, had painted a very grim picture; and he had been far from the only person to think so. It wasn't very long after that when the Resistance learned they'd be getting some special help— but, again, Logan insisted that he'd been talking too much, and with a grand flourish he called the session to an end.

Once these five days had passed, it was time.

Chapter Eleven

For The People!

The morning began with a very distinct feel in the air. It was difficult to put into words, but it felt fiery, electric, and clear all at the same time; energizing, invigorating. This was what a call to arms felt like; of this Jaiden was sure, anyway.

"I do feel nervous," Mishaela said softly. "I know that's only natural, though, so I'll try to power through it. It's like… the morning before an important test. I can do this. I do it often."

"That's it, get in the zone!" Madeline encouraged her. "You've got this!"

"By the way…" Gavin said as he scribbled some notes in a notebook he'd claimed as his own; it had an orange pattern reminiscent of lava. "After considering everything we've learned, I think I have a general idea on what the story behind this place is; however, there's a few pieces I don't quite understand. I'm hoping that we can ask Logan after this whole ordeal has been resolved."

Madeline nodded. "Hopefully things go well enough that we have a chance *to* ask."

"Revolutionary breakfast is ready!" Jaiden said then, bursting into the room. "Nice and full of the right carbs, in case things have to get physical."

"Really?" Mishaela asked, as everyone walked to the kitchen, stunned that her best friend had put so much effort into the meal.

"...No. Sorry. I'm too dumb to calculate carbs at all, let alone remember which ones are the good ones."

The five sat together at the dining table, eating their revolutionary breakfast of pancakes and eggs, realizing this may be the last time they were able to eat together. "Remember the dress code for today," Madeline told everyone. "Express individuality. Bright colors or all black, show some skin— whatever you like. The Resistance has instructed everyone in the village to do the same."

"Wait. If we're essentially wearing whatever we want, shouldn't we be saying there's no dress code?" Jaiden asked.

"Hey, I'm just using the phrasing that was in the official notice." Madeline shrugged. "I didn't write the thing."

Madeline, Jasiela, and Jaiden had already finished dressing. Jaiden had chosen to wear a red lace over-dress with a pink spaghetti strap dress under, and a pink flower in her hair to match. Jasiela wore a pair of blue jeans and a black corset, her hair in a long braid. Madeline had on a pair of black and white checkered shorts and a short-sleeved purple silk blouse.

"I guess this is the last moment of peace we'll have for a little while," Jasiela said then. "We better treasure it."

"Hey, Gavin." Jaiden put her fork down, showing that this was important. "I love Mishaela like a sister, so it *really* does not feel good to think of anything bad happening to her; that being said, if it does, you need to be ready to take over for her. All right?"

Gavin nodded. "I'll do my best and then some," he said. "I think we can agree and only hope that things don't have to come to that, though."

"Absolutely." Jaiden gave him a firm nod in response.

When the girls got back to their room, Mishaela got dressed. She decided to wear a three-quarter sleeve turquoise leopard-print dress with a pair of black sparkly flats, with her hair tied into a messy bun.

"Why are you all staring at me? I...I have a sweater," Mishaela said uneasily. Usually, she wasn't so nervous about showing this fairly modest amount of skin, but these weren't usual circumstances, after all. "Should I wear it?"

"Only if you wanna," Jaiden told her, and she quickly put it on. "It looks like we're going to be running early, by the way. Should we head out early?"

"Eh, I'd say no. If we hang out in the area too long, it makes it more likely for us to get caught or look suspicious," replied Madeline. "I don't think we should arrive in the square any earlier than we need to."

"Right, good point," agreed Jaiden. "Then I guess we're just... here for a little while longer."

"I wonder what the palace looks like inside," Madeline said. "You know, like the interior design."

"There's probably a lot of purple," Gavin responded. "Or burgundy. Maybe even indigo. Historically, those have been common royal colors." He took a short breath. "Hey, as long as we have the time to discuss things, there's something that's been tugging at the back of my mind since we were in the library."

"Yeah?" Jaiden let on.

"I was the one who was in the area of literature where The Dictator first came into power, right?" Gavin asked, thinking of what to say next. "Well, there's... no overlap. What I mean is, I first read one of the short books from around then, and there didn't seem to be any records about him– you know, where and when he was born, his history, if he has any family, anything. That night, when you all fell asleep, I went back and read a few more books to be sure. There's nothing there. Nothing at all."

"Maybe they don't keep records here," Jasiela suggested.

"Mm-mmm." Madeline said. "They do. They're in file cabinets down in the library; I saw them that same day."

"Right, and that was my next stop after I realized something was a bit odd," agreed Gavin. "There's nothing there, either."

"Well, that's strange, then." Jaiden was confused. "One could almost say that he appeared from thin air. Metaphorically, of course, because people can't actually... appear."

"Also, remember what Phoenix said about learning his real name being a crime?" pointed out Mishaela. "It'd make sense for him to destroy all the records of before he came into power, if you take that into account."

"Oh yeah, that makes sense..." Madeline agreed. "Although it makes you wonder why the hell he's so adamant about no one learning his name."

All the teens thought about that, but ended up collectively shrugging and going back to the puzzle. After it had been completed and put away, Gavin supportively placed his hand on Mishaela's shoulder. "Are you ready?" he asked her.

She nodded, nervously. "I have this weird feeling, though," she said, her voice a little shaky. "Like something's going to happen, you know?"

"Remember, though, we're there," Gavin reminded her. "And if things start to go badly, we have the Resistance. You'll be okay. Okay?"

Mishaela nodded. "I place faith in your ability to be good guards," she said, smiling at everyone.

"After all, Logan's training couldn't have just amounted to nothing like that," added Jaiden. "Come on! My legs feel extra strong now. Literally ready to kick some ass."

Everyone laughed at that. "Are we still running early?" Mishaela asked.

Madeline motioned as if she was going to check her phone, but then stopped herself and looked at the clock in the room. "A little, but I think now is a good time to start heading that way. Let's go kiddos!"

"Kiddos?" Jasiela frowned. "We're the same age."

"Don't worry about that, and come on! We can't be late," Madeline reminded everyone. "Make sure to grab your cloaks so we can get into the square undetected."

"Right." Jaiden reached for hers.

Perhaps the most tense moment of this excursion so far was the examination by the guards at the entrance to the square. Once it was over, Madeline almost asked what it was they were looking for (because this search, once again, was brief and not exactly thorough) but held her tongue, not wanting the group to seem too suspicious.

"How we doing on time?" Jasiela asked.

"Five minutes early," replied Madeline. "That's enough time to find our compadres, don't you think? It's not a huge area."

"Agreed," Jaiden nodded. "Toward the palace, then?"

"Yep, toward the palace," replied Madeline. "We should find our friends there."

Arriving at the square near the front of the palace, the teens found the head of the Resistance, dressed in ordinary clothes. There were a decent number of civilians around as well, but they all still wore their cloaks and other conservative clothing. Thunder tipped his hat to the group, his cowboy attire a bit shocking at first glance; but, somehow it complemented his low ponytail of locs. The whole look felt very authentic, as if this would be the way one would encounter Thunder in a more normal and modern setting.

"Feels good to get out in normal clothes again, wouldn't you say?" he asked when the teens were close enough to hear.

"Normal?" Jaiden stared at his fringe jacket, chaps, and spurs.

"Probably not the best choice of words, I'll admit. But what can I say? True normality is boring." Thunder laughed.

"I am right there with you, my man!" agreed Madeline. "But how did you get through without causing a ruckus? You are probably breaking every rule of the dress code right now with that getup."

Thunder laughed at this assessment. "I can't be telling y'all all my secrets! I'd be a lot less interesting if I did that. Well, then. Y'all found the place okay, so lead the way, ladies and gentleman. Which route do we take?"

"Uh, I'm not— never mind, not important," Jaiden retracted her complaint. With this, everyone looked at Madeline; since she was the oldest, she'd quickly become the spokesperson for the group of teenagers.

"How about we just march right up to the front door," she replied.

Thunder nodded, and held his hand up, waving it toward the direction of the palace. "Onward."

And so, the entire group set off.

"How far is it?" Jaiden asked.

"It's right over there." Thunder pointed to the tall, tiered dome building drawing closer on the horizon. "It should take about three minutes to get there. But it has a lofty flight of stairs, which should take another three."

"Three whole minutes walking up stairs?" Gavin complained.

"For me, yes," Thunder replied, "But as you can see, I'm kind of getting on in my years. It shouldn't really be a problem for you young, strappin' five."

"I hope not." Gavin looked genuinely worried.

"I sincerely hope you don't get tired just from walking up stairs." Logan appeared with a wave. "Won't we need your strength as a precaution?"

"Logan!" Jasiela said then. He was dressed almost exactly the same as he had been when they'd first met, except his pants were an emerald green. It was another hot day, so his lack of shirt probably helped with not only mobility, but comfort as well.

"Onward and upward, my friends," he said. "I have nothing but the utmost confidence in you all. After all, your appearance here was ordained."

"Logan," Thunder said, a bit of warning in his voice.

"Right." He nodded. "Well, at any rate, everyone in the combat team is in place and things seem to be moving smoothly, so that's why I'm here! Plus, there's strength in numbers, right?"

The group arrived at the base of the stairs then. The stairs were well-built and very fancy, to be sure, but this was also more stairs than any of the teens would have cared to climb, even on a good day.

Fortunately, they'd all worn comfortable shoes.

"Is it time?" Gavin asked.

Logan was the first to survey the area. "As expected, the nearest guard at ground level seems to be that gentleman over there," he nodded toward where a guard was pointing toward a building, probably giving directions. "His back is to us, but if it begins to get noticeably loud, he'll definitely hear."

Thunder smirked. "Good."

He nodded once, and the people nearest them reached for the necks of their cloaks, ready to unfasten them easily. After a moment more of tense silence, they began to pull them away, tossing the fabric aside and yelling in encouragement for those in the area to do the same. It wasn't long before the guard noticed, and began to call for reinforcements.

"That's my cue," Logan said then, already heading toward the crowd, farther away from the palace.

"Logan! What are you doing?!" Madeline asked.

"Don't worry!" He turned back. "Tudo bem. All part of the plan!"

"He knows what he's doing," Thunder said reassuringly. "Logan's been preparing for something like this for a long time. He wouldn't go into a situation half-cocked, so try not to worry too much about him."

"I guess..." Jaiden replied.

"Anyway, I reckon this is where we part ways," Thunder said, stepping in front of the group. He took off his hat and held it to his chest, facing Mishaela. "We really do appreciate what you're doing for our people, Miss Pagliardi," he said humbly.

She smiled, a small blush in her cheeks. "It's not just me," she said. "All of us are contributing in some way. And please just call me Mishaela. You're being way too formal."

"Of course, Mishaela," Thunder said, returning his hat to his head. "We wish you the best, of course." He held out his hand toward the palace entrance. "Now, if the ruckus has been goin' on this long with no appearance from anyone in the palace, we can forget about forcing a public game. Y'all might wanna get moving before them guards realize this is where the whole ruckus started. Don't need them slowin' you down."

Mishaela smiled again, and began to walk. "Right. Let's get going, guys," she beckoned her teammates. They followed, none of them seeming particularly excited to do so— not that they should, given the circumstances.

From the perspective at the top of the stairs, the sounds of the crowd at the foot of the palace had diminished so much that it was almost quiet; a small murmur of activity amidst the tense silence. "Do we just walk inside?" asked Gavin once they'd all reached the top, pushing the front door open slightly. "You'd think there would be more security than that. For one, weren't there supposed to be guards here?"

"Well, according to Phoenix, the immediate areas of the castle are pretty much public, like a museum. Probably to show off all the wealth," Madeline rolled her eyes. "There were indeed supposed to be guards here, though. I wonder why they're not here now?"

"They may have moved farther in," suggested Jaiden. "Some kind of precautionary repositioning when they noticed the people congregating outside?"

"Mm. Possible, I suppose." Madeline nodded. "But I think we should get going before things start getting too complicated down there. From here, we continue straight on to get to the area where we request an audience."

"That's easier than expected, if I'm being honest," Jasiela said as everyone walked in. "Takes a bit of the stress off. Just a bit."

The corridors of the palace were indeed burgundy, as Gavin had projected; the color matched the strip of carpet that the five were walking on to guide them to the royal chamber. The actual floor was checked black and white, almost as if it were designed that way to foreshadow the games of chess that would be played. There was also a peculiar scent within; not anything repulsive, or even off-putting, but pointedly noticeable. Jaiden felt as though she had smelled it somewhere before, but she couldn't quite place where or when.

As Madeline had explained, it was a straight walk to the throne room, where— surprisingly— there were only four guards at the doorway, two on either side, in their typical mulberry uniforms. It was here that the teens finally came face-to-face with The Dictator, and a couple more guards flanking his throne; these had uniforms of a darker mulberry tone, and gold shoulder pauldrons. They seemed to be of a higher rank, due to the additional details.

It was strange– in person, The Dictator didn't look as though he was out of his twenties, and was a lot more attractive than the very unflattering picture of him that was in every book. His eyes didn't look shifty, so much as calculating or cautious. His dark curls were almost beautiful— and all five of the guests in this palace would venture that he thought the same.

"Oh. *There* they are." Madeline gestured toward the guards.

"Ah, there are the visitors. So I see you've finally arrived." The Dictator rose from his throne, and walked a few paces closer to the group, probably to be able to hear and speak to them more easily. His voice wasn't loud or commanding, like one would expect of someone in his position; while there was the clear presence of bass tones, his words floated through the air, like they were a balloon without a weight, or an empty bag. "I've been expecting you."

"Have you?" Madeline said flatly.

"Of course. One would have to be unable to hear, to not notice the din outside. It was only a matter of time before someone showed up."

One of the guards hastily raised his shotgun, but The Dictator held out a hand to stop him. "Stand down. This may be interesting." He then asked, "Of course, just because I knew this meeting was coming, that's not to say I know everything about its purpose. To what do I owe this visit?"

"A game of chess, primarily," Mishaela replied, confidently stepping forward. "Flustered chess, that is; the game you created. I want to be your opponent."

"You?" He started to laugh, but abruptly stopped himself. "Interesting. If you've taken the time to learn about our customs, though, then I suspect that you didn't come here for just a friendly game of chess. Your wager?"

"On behalf of the people, we want you to vacate." Mishaela took a breath. "In other words, if I win, you have to give control of the village back to the people."

The Dictator paused for a moment, hand under his chin, before beginning to pace around the room. "Control of the village to the people?" he repeated. "I see. That is a hefty demand, for you see, I've grown quite fond of this land of mine. I'm sure you can agree that it is quite a grand place, even with its current lack of color and wildlife? It's... admirable, you coming in here with such bold demands. Do you even know the depths of that which you ask? Nevertheless, it certainly makes things *interesting*. I suppose... seeing that I won't lose, there should be no harm in taking on your challenge. But!" He stepped closer to Mishaela, a cunning grin upon his face. "I'm sure that, even at your age, you're aware that it's in poor form to have a one-sided bet."

"Truly." Mishaela nodded.

"As such, I'll place a wager as well. If I win... ah, 'if I win.' Such uncertain statements are unbecoming of one as absolute as I. Obviously, upon my victory, I shall retain my position of power. In addition, you all will never set foot in this country again— no, most of you will not, except for *you*, young lady. I get to take you away from you little rebel friends, and use you however I see fit."

Mishaela looked terrified.

"Talk about bold," Jasiela said then to the remaining three people near her. "...Although, I guess it *would* kinda be an equivalent exchange."

"What do you mean, equivalent exchange?" Gavin asked her. "The whole purpose of us doing this is so that there won't be anyone being scrutinized anymore; to have to surrender a person as if they're property squanders the very principle!"

While that conversation was going on, Jaiden suddenly had another very strong premonition, as her sight fell to a curtain. Waiting for a chance to step away unnoticed, she stealthily tiptoed over and upon pulling the curtain back, found a hidden lever. She put her hand on it, preparing to pull it, but something— this tiny voice from nowhere— whispered to her.

Don't pull it. Break it. Render it unusable.

"How the hell do I do that?" Jaiden said softly, immediately checking to be sure no one heard her, but it appeared that the guards in the immediate area were now busy with preparing the area for the impending game of chess. She knew she didn't have a lot of time to pull this off, so she placed a hand on the lever again and forced it the wrong way as forcefully as she could, hoping that— *snap.*

"Ah." Sometimes, the best solution really was the simplest one.

She returned to the others just as four of the guards returned with some documents, a table, and a couple of chairs. The Dictator had sent off the remaining two guards to bring a chess board for the game. "It may seem cumbersome, but I did not become successful without learning that one must procure any agreements in writing. Let's begin in just a moment. While you're signing that, there is one more precaution I must take," he said then, and set off in the direction that Jaiden had just come from. "What the?! Where is my..."

"Looking for this?" Jaiden inquired, holding up the other end of the broken lever. "Sorry about that, bro, but we can't just give our friend away like that. Looks like we'll be playing fair today."

At first The Dictator looked furious, then his eyes widened as he looked from Jaiden to Mishaela, then back to Jaiden. He raised a finger, pointing at Jaiden. "You're the one whose sight is aided by the goddesses, but you're not the one who will be playing." He laughed then, the sinister sound echoing down the halls of the palace. "Yes, today, we shall play fair; quite so."

The grin on his face made Jaiden very suspicious; suspicious, and worried.

"The goddesses?" she whispered. "What is he talking about? Madeline, do you know— was that mentioned in one of your books?"

She paused, thinking. "From what I remember, there are a few books here that mention something kinda like that," she explained. "As it goes, every now and then, the goddesses are said to give people an enhancement on their regular abilities, to help with things that they can't interfere with personally. I didn't bring it up 'cause at the time it didn't seem relevant. I'm sorry! If I had known..."

That meant that all this time, the goddesses had been the ones helping Jaiden see things that she normally wouldn't. It dawned on her then that, had she been the one to play the game of flustered chess, the goddesses would have helped her win; and judging by his reaction, it was clear that The Dictator knew that too.

The one time I decide to keep quiet in my entire fourteen years of living, and it comes back to bite me. If I'd mentioned these premonitions before, we probably would've reached this conclusion before now, and there'd be no rush involved. Jaiden sighed internally.

But now I do wonder why the goddesses can't get involved.

"Don't apologize, Madeline. You did what you felt you needed to, with the information you had. I can't be mad at you for that."

The board and pieces that the servants brought back were stunning; the board was made of marble, its black and white squares glistening in the light flowing in from the windows behind the throne. The playing pieces were made of thin, clear glass, and were filled with some clear, viscous liquid and iridescent glitter. "Mishaela, correct?" The Dictator asked, to which she nodded.

"Have a seat, then."

She sat in one of the chairs, and no sooner had she done so, had the glitter inside the pieces on her side turned pink. When The Dictator sat, the glitter within his pieces turned dark purple. After a sporting handshake, and a moment's glance, the game began; all six of the guards taking post at the doorway leading to the main corridor, the way that the five had come in.

When the game began, it was deathly quiet, and it continued this way for a few moments, a few moves occurring during this time; none without a period of consideration.

"It would seem that I chose a rather appropriate set for today's game," were The Dictator's first words to pierce the silence.

"Hm." Mishaela tried to conceal her intrigue.

"I'm sure you're curious as to what I mean by that: the board is made of the same marble as the floors of this palace. Marble is native to this area... or perhaps was. But its disappearance was a natural occurrence, one unaided by men. Nothing here is ever solely the product of man, not even my rule."

"Huh." Mishaela nodded. "What is that supposed to mean?"

"Exactly what it appears to. It's not like one ever aspires to rule a kingdom from birth."

"I don't know. Back home, that's kinda debatable," pointed out Jaiden.

"So it is." The Dictator moved one of his pawns. "In those days, there was no ruler, did you know that? Oh, but I'm sure your Resistance friends probably told you of those times. It... worked, I suppose. To see a society conduct itself, with no governing force, was honestly quite fascinating, with how well it sustained itself. Be that as it may, it wasn't always that way. That's something you likely *didn't* know."

A silence passed then, upon Mishaela's turn.

"One can hardly tell upon looking at it now, but this is the capital of the nation that it stands within. Shocking, I'm sure. This colorless land of desolation? But this land prospered when it was directly governed by the goddesses."

"It was?" Madeline asked.

"Of course. This world is their creation. One owns that which they create," The Dictator replied. "I suppose it is because of their inability to maintain permanent corporeal forms that they vacated such a direct level of involvement, but no one can say for certain. This marked the start of the anarchy era, but it is also when the decline of this world began. This seems to be the only area that never stabilized after a certain point, and continued to decline. There's not a soul who knows why, but... when it became well-known that this land would not stabilize, it was my duty to assume a position of power."

"But why... was it *your* duty?" Mishaela asked hesitantly. "Why not anyone else?"

"Can you not understand that it was my calling? If anyone else aspired, why didn't they move?"

Whenever the remaining group was unsure of how the game was going (which would mean for most of its duration) they'd turn to look at Gavin. They could tell by his facial expression who was winning. A major wave of relief washed over the three of them at this point: when his worried frown, which he'd worn since the outset, began to turn into a somewhat satisfied smirk.

The guy might need to take his own advice about poker faces, thought Madeline.

That particular aroma that Jaiden had smelled when the group had first entered seemed to be stronger now. She noticed this because she'd formerly gotten to the point where she didn't notice it, but it now felt as though they'd gotten closer to the source— except no one had moved for the better part of twenty minutes.

It became clear not very long after this realization, that Jaiden noticed Mishaela was winning the game. Jasiela and Gavin held her hands tightly in anticipation.

"Surely you cannot fault a man who wants to preserve his land. It was a losing battle, this we all knew, but to give the people hope meant there would need to be no chance the anarchy would ever become unstable again. So if I had to squash a few liberties... it was only ever for preservation of life as we were owed. As it was at the time of this world's creation."

The Dictator drummed his fingers on the table. It was his move, and the room was so quiet that one could hear the sounds of the guards walking outside the throne room. "You are a worthy adversary, Mishaela Pagliardi. Yes, very worthy indeed..."

He moved his jester piece.

"But I will not be defeated on this day."

Mishaela's response was to look up, and that's when her friends noticed her face had gone red.

"Whoa, hey, that is a concerning amount of red," whispered Jasiela. "What's going on, do you guys know?"

"I don't. But this isn't a good time for it, whatever it is," Jaiden also whispered, in a hurried, anxious manner. "What do we do? What *can* we do? You know some basic med stuff, right, Madeline?"

"I don't think this particular thing is within my knowledge banks," she replied.

"Not to interrupt a quite serious matter, but..." Gavin furrowed his brow, sniffing. "Does it smell a bit melon-y in here to you, girls?"

Jaiden's eyes bulged in shock. Upon Gavin asking that, and seeing that Mishaela's hands were also red, she realized what the aroma was that she'd been noticing this whole time.

Cantaloupe.

As Jaiden realized this, the smell grew louder, seemingly pulsating out of the walls. It took a heavy toll on Mishaela, who was now too weak to move her pieces very far. The Dictator chuckled softly, not quite loud enough for anyone but Mishaela to hear, as he frivolously moved his pieces in the checkers manner, no longer paying much attention to the game, in a showboating manner.

In his mind, this game was as good as won.

"So weak," he said, the disgust radiating off of his words, before adapting a sickeningly sweet tone. "This game may have been an intriguing diversion in the beginning, but now it's beginning to bore me. You know, at this very moment, it isn't too late for you to forfeit. My staff can get rid of that nasty rash you're getting, and you'll have a fresh start to your life here. And don't worry—" he flashed the others a smug smile— "I'll take good care of her."

"Fix this! What's wrong with her?" Jasiela asked Jaiden frantically, grabbing her and lightly shaking her for added effect.

Jaiden pointed up, waving her finger in a circle, in the stagnant air. "Cantaloupe," she said. "She's allergic. It makes her break out like this, but I've never seen her get so weak from it. Probably the prolonged exposure."

"Shit." Jasiela sighed. "God damn it! Why didn't you tell us about this before?!"

"How could I have possibly been able to predict that a *cantaloupe allergy* would be our biggest problem?!"

"I will admit, you lasted longer than I thought you would," The Dictator continued. "I wanted to get rid of you before you even made it into my throne room, but I suppose this has been nice, in a way. It gets boring after a time, playing opponents that have no chance of winning. A challenge was long overdue. Besides, if you had never made it here, I never would have been able to see how alluring you are, now would I?" He smiled evilly, an obvious gloat. "I had considered having you here would be beneficial; to use your obvious intellect in conjunction with my own to perhaps bring prosperity to the land; but now, I can also have you here as my pet."

"You... you creep! You can't do this!" Jaiden yelled, only resisting the urge to clock him then and there when she heard the guards behind her, moving to grab their weapons.

"Oh, can't I?" he asked, smugly, as he stood. "Why not? This is my palace, my kingdom, and my infinite reign. I do believe that there is nothing that can stop me from doing anything I want. I will concede that there have been a few who have tried to change that before you, but they've all been unsuccessful. Their approaches were so haphazardly put together that it's been almost amusing to watch their failed attempts over and over... and over." He sat back down again, not looking as he moved another piece on the chessboard, just for fun. He then laughed, the sound echoing down the halls once again. "Foolish rebels. As if a group of teenagers could overpower me; and why would you aim to? Do you not understand the prosperity I'll bring to this land; why do you wish to? What do you have to say for yourselves?"

All four teens had a few choice words in their minds, surely. Jaiden, in particular, was just getting ready to unleash a flurry of things that, had she said them in front of her parents, would have made them denounce her as a Winchester— but she stopped, seeing Mishaela's hand finally feebly pick up a piece and move it.

The dark purple king was trapped.

"Check...mate," she said weakly.

Chapter Twelve

Defeat

"N ooooooooo!" The Dictator screamed at the top of his lungs.

As he approached his latter "os," a thin cloud of black smoke began to circulate around his body, and the ground began to tremble. It was such an inconsequential tremor initially that it seemed imaginary, but then it began to rumble more powerfully, to the point where it was difficult to keep one's footing.

The guards ran out of the room, likely either afraid or for backup.

"So help me, if this rumble is the castle collapsing, what kinda cliche adventure video game shit—" started Jasiela.

"I don't think that's it! The tremor feels more atmospheric than foundational!" replied Gavin.

"I'm not even gonna pretend I know what that means, Gavin."

Any response that Gavin could have prepared was interrupted as Jaiden quickly leapt at him to push him aside in barely enough time to avoid the lunge from The Dictator; he then attempted to lunge again, but Madeline pulled Jasiela out of the way; she quickly turned and readied a retaliating kick, but was knocked off balance when her leg phased through The Dictator's corporeal form.

"What?! This cannot be! I am immortal! I am eternal! I am..."

Suddenly, The Dictator's body began to crumble, like dry leaves on a cold fall day; more smoke erupted from the core of his body, engulfing the entirety of the room. For a while, there was nothing else in the room. There was no sound, no space, no time. There was only black smoke.

And then, there was nothing.

The Dictator was no more.

After regaining her footing, Jasiela cautiously walked toward the pile of ash-like substance where he'd stood, trying to understand what had just happened. "He... it's like he just... he imploded." She turned back toward the group.

"Well, I certainly can't say I was expecting *that*." Gavin grimaced.

"You're telling me," Jaiden agreed, pretty traumatized by what she'd just seen.

For a moment, the four stood there, taking in what had just happened. There was nothing but a pile of black ashes, where a human had once stood.

Or had it? *Had* this man been completely human?

Jaiden's head turned, then, to a small hand near the ashes. "Mishaela!" She turned to the others. "Let's open up some windows in here, guys, get some fresh air going! Somebody should probably take care of the ashy stuff too; we can't be too careful."

Madeline glanced around the room before seeing a small, golden vase nearby. Quickly grabbing it, she said, "I'll take care of the ashes!"

The rest frantically ran to open the windows of the throne room. "Is she going to be all right, Jaiden?" asked Gavin.

"I don't know," she replied truthfully. She could only recall one time in their lives where Mishaela's allergy had been provoked: the day that they found out it existed. They were in the sixth grade, and they'd gone to a picnic for a field trip. There had been a boy, one of their classmates whose name Jaiden couldn't even remember at this point, who had asked Mishaela to hold his bowl of fruit salad— and being the kind person she was, she had agreed. Faster than one could say "what's in this salad?" her arms had broken out into a fiery-red rash.

Needless to say, neither ever saw the boy again after that day.

Madeline had swept all the ashes into the vase she had picked up, and after she did that, the smell seemed to begin to wane. Jaiden sprinted over to Mishaela once she, Gavin, and Jasiela had opened all the windows in the room, lifting her head off of the table. "Mishaela, wake up!" she practically yelled. "You're all right! The cantaloupe is gone! Breathe!"

Her face had begun to turn back to its normal color, but the rash still prevailed on her arms, legs, and chest areas. The rest of the group congregated around the two girls. "Why don't we get her closer to the windows?" Madeline suggested. "Cleaner air. That should help speed up the process, right? Somebody help me out here."

She and Gavin lifted her and carefully, but hastily, moved toward the open windows. Jasiela followed, then Jaiden. After a few tense moments in the vicinity of the open windows, Mishaela took a huge, awkward breath, coming to.

"She's okay!" Jasiela said, relieved, a hand to her chest.

After a few smaller breaths, Mishaela was up to speaking. She asked, "Did I... do it?"

"What? Oh! Yes, yes you did it!" Madeline said, giving her a huge smile. "You won! That guy is history!"

"The village is no longer oppressed," Jaiden added.

"It belongs to the people," Gavin finished.

She nodded slightly. "That's... that's good. Very good. I'm happy."

Mishaela turned to Gavin then. "I guess you won't need to play today after all."

She managed to give him a weak smile before going completely limp, fainting into his arms.

"The fresh air from the windows is beneficial, but if we truly want Mishaela to recover, we should probably make good our escape now," Gavin said then.

It was then that everyone's heads turned to the entrance of the throne room, suddenly hearing footsteps fast approaching. "...However, I suppose we shan't discount the possibility of there still being guards and concierges within."

"Well, crap." Madeline sighed. "If it's not one thing, it's another. We got a plan, guys?"

"Hey, don't worry, we got this," Jasiela said. "I'll help Gavin support Mishaela's weight. Madeline, Jaiden, I hope you guys' practice with Logan came in handy, because we'll need you to force our way if we run into any lackeys."

"I'm ready," agreed Jaiden determinedly.

"Same here. We'll lead the way," added Madeline.

The group rushed through the arch of the throne room, in the process knocking back a few guards that had been lurking just outside. However, there was a horde of guards further back; an uncountable number.

The memories of Logan's tutelage were flowing through Jaiden's mind now: if one didn't have time to warm up before needing to fight, start with quick moves meant to stagger the enemy and then progress to stronger, more potent moves. The smaller, quick moves were more efficient when working to stun an opponent; there soon began an unspoken strategy for Jaiden to stun someone and Madeline— being the stronger one of the two— to follow up and incapacitate them with the time that had been bought.

The numbers, though intimidating at first, began to work against the enemy forces in that when they tried to crowd into the main hallway, it was easy to knock over multiple people with one hit. This was what made an escape possible at all, if any of the five were to look back at the moment through an analytic lense.

It wasn't a pretty escape— sometimes a stray fighter would be able to break through the frontrunners' defense, and Gavin had been kicked in the face at least once— but, after what felt like just over the amount of fighting the two could handle, Madeline was the first that crashed through the main palace doors. Being met with cheers from the majority of the crowd at the foot of the stairs, none of the teens thought of basking in their victory, too concerned with the task at hand. They had to get down these stairs and get the help they needed.

"Oh boy. Forgot about the stairs." Jaiden looked down.

"I got it! Guys, help me get Mishaela onto my back; I can take her from here," volunteered Madeline.

"You just deadass got through punching at least 20 guys in the face; no way," Jasiela replied. "You need rest."

"Don't worry about that! I got this!" Madeline insisted. "You guys need to clear a path so we can get through all this confusion."

"She's right," Gavin agreed. "There's a lot of people down there; a lot of confusion it looks like, as well."

"Right. So let's go," replied Madeline, getting into position to hoist Mishaela onto her back. "Jaiden, can you watch my back in case someone comes out of the palace?"

"Yo." She immediately assumed her position as they all started down the stairs, barreling down each step as fast as they could without losing their footing. Somehow, this trip felt longer than going up the stairs had, but that could just be because the situation somehow felt more dire than it had before, now that one of their own was incapacitated. Madeline began to scan the crowd for familiar faces as she got close enough to be able to discern them, and felt a wave of relief so strong it almost knocked her off her feet, when she finally saw Thunder again.

"Is everyone okay?" asked Thunder, as the teens came into earshot. He was still stationed right at the base of the stairs, making sure the situation outside didn't become so rowdy that it disrupted the plan.

"We need some medical attention for Mishaela," replied Jasiela, as Madeline carefully handed her over to Thunder. "Just to be on the safe side, we should all probably get checked out too, since that was a rough exit. But her first!"

"Of course." Thunder nodded, securing Mishaela on his own back. "Logan!"

Logan called out indistinctly in the distance... somewhere.

"Find your sister and tell her to bring her group of medics to the old base!" Thunder replied.

Logan yelled again, seemingly in the affirmative.

"We're on it. The rest of you, stay close to me," Thunder instructed then. "I know you're all exhausted, but we can't have you gettin' separated among all these people. We need to get you back safely."

"Got it. Everyone, grab on," Madeline held out her hand. Gavin grabbed it, then he reached for Jasiela's hand with his other, and with her other hand, she tightly clutched the hand of Jaiden.

They could celebrate later. For now, getting out of here in one piece— and securing their health— was more important.

Chapter Thirteen

I Hate Goodbyes

"She'll be fine," Phoenix reassured the worried group of teens, who had congregated around the bed that Mishaela currently rested in. "She just needs a bit of rest, and some of the boys should be here soon with the herbs I need to make the treatment for her skin."

Now that no one had to be covered completely, it was more noticeable that Phoenix was also not very much older than the teens, and was much prettier than the country's former dress code had let on. Her curly black hair tumbled past her shoulders in an almost unreal way, kind of like how the women in advertisements for curly hair care products always had the most perfectly defined and hydrated curls. It was also extremely obvious, now, that she and Logan were related. Their similar dark hair, facial structure, and eye shapes were the biggest giveaway.

As it turned out, in addition to being their executive planner, she was also the Resistance's head medic, which was why she was the person currently overseeing Mishaela's recuperation.

"That's a relief. Thank you for everything you're doing, Phoenix," Madeline said then.

"It's my job to treat any of the Resistance's members; and what are you all, if not part of our family? I know you all have already been seen, but is there anything else we can get you, while you wait?"

Phoenix asked then. "It's the least we can do, after everything you've done for us."

"Oh, may I have another cold compress, then?" asked Gavin, who was currently holding one to his jaw, right where he'd gotten kicked. "This one's getting warm."

"I'd like one for each of my feet too, if it's not too much trouble," added Madeline. "After all those kicks? Hurts like a *mother*."

Phoenix laughed. "It'll be no problem at all. I'll be right back."

"Might I commend you on a job well done?" a familiar voice asked once she'd left.

Everyone turned, to see a familiar figure dressed in her familiar exquisite silky clothes; this time, it was a peach-toned dress with long sleeves that reached her ankles. Instead of her usual unreadable expression, she was smiling, which made her look much older than she did previously; but in a warm, welcoming way, like one's kind elderly neighbor.

Madeline gasped. "Laelia!" she said. "Hey! Where've you been? You just plunked us here and then disappeared! You could've told us that Jaiden could see things we can't, or that The Dictator would play on Mishaela's allergy, or... or..."

A short silence followed.

"You seem to have done just fine without knowing any of that," Laelia said.

Madeline nodded. "I... guess you have a point. So why are you here now, then?"

She picked up the vase, in which the black dust was contained. "For this. The goddesses want to ensure he never returns. Of course, that's largely thanks to you five. Nothing we do will ever be enough."

"Aw, come on, you're embarrassing us," Jasiela said modestly.

"She is right, though," agreed Phoenix, as she re-entered the room. "We'll never be able to appropriately thank you."

The room became silent for a moment then.

"Hey, so, what's the deal with all this talk of goddesses and stuff anyway?" Jasiela asked. "The creation of this place, the decline of the city, all that? Are we really in a completely different world than the one we usually live in?"

"And is magic really real?" Madeline added.

Laelia smiled. "I think you all already know the answers to those questions."

"I can guarantee we don't, but you're just gonna sidestep us on this, huh." Jasiela poured.

"Should you wish to know, there is one here that can give you the knowledge you seek- as long as she is permitted to." Laelia gave a nod to Phoenix, and then pointed toward the door. "Once Mishaela is well again, and you've said your good-byes, I have made it so that you can leave through either the front or back door. I trust you're ready to get back to your families."

It was true. Madeline missed her sisters, and Jaiden was wondering how her parents were coping with her being gone. Even Gavin was beginning to miss the noise of his home, the noise that he'd complained about when he'd first arrived here. It was funny, the things one started to miss when they no longer had them.

"By the way..." Laelia said then. "All of you, including you, Phoenix. The youth... you ask a lot of questions. Some may try to frame this as a bad thing, but I do not believe that it is so. You all should continue with this inquisitive spirit; to question everything, even life as you know it. One never knows what one doesn't know, until they begin to ask questions."

Laelia departed then, through the door.

"Is that— is that the first time we've seen her actually use the door?" Jaiden asked with a chuckle.

Almost instantly after Laelia's departure, a man dressed in a simple t-shirt and pants, both black, walked in with a small bag of herbs. "Here's the plants you were looking for, ma'am."

"Ah, yes," Phoenix said, with a nod, as she stood. "I'll be back; I have to go prepare these."

Both she and the man left the room then. The room became silent, with the exception of the ticking clock mounted on the far side of the room. There was a significant amount of tension in the air, no one knowing what to say or do while their friend was in the bed unconscious. What was there to say, in situations like this? It somehow didn't feel right to carry on as normal, but to continue to discuss the situation at hand also felt wrong somehow; it would just stress everyone out.

After a few moments more, Mishaela stirred, and everyone immediately turned to look at her. "Where... where am I?" she asked, softly; weakly, as if her throat was sore. There was a good chance it was, after all.

"Back at base, in Gavin's bed," Madeline replied. "How are you feeling?"

Mishaela's response was to rub her arm. "Why does my skin hurt?"

Jaiden smiled. "Don't worry about that. It'll be gone soon." She then grabbed her hand. "Mishaela, you're officially a revolutionary. If not for you, we wouldn't have won."

She shook her head, denying this claim. "I'd have never been able to do so if it wasn't for you all. Come *on*, all this flattery isn't good for my usually humble personality."

"I guess you're right," Jasiela agreed, chuckling. "I'm not sure you'd have had the advantage you did if Gavin hadn't pointed out the smell... and if Jaiden hadn't been so bold to argue with the guy, buying you time."

Jaiden laughed in response. "So I guess we did all help in our own way!"

"Yes, we all did," Mishaela said contentedly. She then paused, to put her arms around her stomach. "...Guys? I'm hungry."

Everyone in the room laughed.

"Maybe one more meal together wouldn't hurt," Madeline agreed.

Phoenix returned with the medicine then. "It's good to see you awake and with your wits about you, Mishaela."

"It's good to be so," she replied. "Thank you for taking care of me."

"As a medic, it would be unbecoming if I didn't." Phoenix held up the jar of medicine, which seemed to be in the form of some type of lotion, a buttery off-white color and with scents of mint, rose, and other aromas that were difficult to place. It was amazing; it worked almost instantly. Mishaela's skin went back to its smooth, creamy normal state in a matter of seconds.

"Thank you," she said politely.

"It's the least I can do." Phoenix sighed sadly. "So, I guess this is the last I'll be seeing of you five."

Madeline nodded somberly. "But there's an upside to that," she told her. "I would assume that, if we never come back, it means the village is in good standing. Right?"

"You're right," Phoenix agreed. "That's a good point. Well, if this is really it, then I should say now that it was a pleasure knowing you all."

"Same here!" agreed Jasiela. "Take it easy, guys. Could you say goodbye to everyone for us, since leaving the house is supposed to take us home?"

"Of course. Logan's going to be sad that you had to leave before he could see you again, but I'm sure he'll understand." Phoenix laughed a little.

"Guess we won't be getting that comprehensive lesson after all," Madeline sighed.

"While I can't give you as comprehensive a lesson as my brother, since I was the reason he wasn't allowed to tell you all the things you wanted to know..." Phoenix smiled. "Magic is a part of our lives here. It's the lifeblood of our land, and to some extent, of ourselves. It is the very composition of our world. Have you touched any of the few plants that are still around, for example? That's the easiest way to tell."

This immediately summoned a memory forth, in Mishaela's mind. "Oh! The golden dust from that rose petal I held that time! So *that* was what that was."

Phoenix nodded. "That's right. Our world is much too complex to explain to you all in one sitting, but I do hope that someday, a day will come where you get to learn everything you've wondered about during your stay. Let's hope it's not under similar circumstances."

"If so, I will personally kick the next dictator's ass," promised Jaiden.

"Not if we get to him first." Phoenix waved to the group, and walked out of the door. "Travel safely!"

"Bye!" everyone said together.

After Phoenix had gone, it seemed like as good a time as any to eat before leaving. And so, everyone flocked to the kitchen, rummaging around a bit before collectively deciding that sandwiches were the best choice to make; simple and quick, to both prepare and eat. They did so in the kitchen; it made sense to do so since there was a small table there, and it was where the sandwiches had to be made in the first place.

"I wonder how much time has passed back home," Gavin said.

After all, Mishaela's iPod had died soon after they'd viewed it that first time. They had learned before that happened, that time did pass here, but at a slower rate. Still, they'd been in this world for more than a week after Gavin's arrival, so a considerable amount of time had to have passed in their own hometowns even with its slower progression.

"I hope not a lot," Madeline said. "If you recall, I've been here the longest. I don't want to get *too* far behind on my schoolwork."

Jaiden smiled. Soon she'd be back in her house, going to school, having regular fights with her parents all over again, like nothing had ever happened. But at the same time, she also felt a tinge of sadness. The chances were slim that she'd ever see Jasiela and Gavin again, and she'd come to think of both of them as friends. Even if they did keep in touch online— and the chances were high that they would— she knew her parents would never let her go to New York or London to visit her newfound friends.

Gavin noticed her silence. "Is something the matter?" he asked.

She nodded. "I'll miss you and Jasiela," she replied. "There's no way to know if we'll ever see each other again."

As a response, Gavin's head sank. "Yeah, I'm not really ready for home myself," he agreed. "I feel kind of important here, you know? And I'm in good company. You, and Madeline, Jasiela, Mishaela."

His facial expression became even sadder, from recounting everyone.

"You lot are the first friends I've ever made outside of circumstance— well, not entirely, but what I mean is... excuse me, I think I need a bit of fresh air," he said, rising from the table.

When he left, the remaining four decided it was time for them to prepare to start making tracks as well. Jaiden walked through the halls slowly, reluctantly. She had never noticed how many chess boards were in this place; they were all unique and exquisite in their own ways, whether it be their boards, their pieces, or a combination of the two. The sight of them all almost made her almost want to learn to play.

No, she countered in her mind, *I'll leave the chess games to the smart people.*

She arrived in her room, and put all of her belongings into her bag that she'd found in the closet. The group was allowed to keep a few of the clothes according to the Resistance, since they'd expressed plans to put this building to use somehow, which was an upside. She checked a second time, making sure she hadn't forgotten anything, before heading out.

Everyone reconvened in the courtyard. The sun was shining brighter than it had at all the entire duration of the teens' stay, and fluffy clouds blew along the sky. It was as if a brand new day had bloomed for this village.

They'd exit through the main back door.

"So... I guess this is good-bye," Jasiela said softly.

"Yeah. I guess so." Jaiden agreed. She hated this feeling of having to fight tears. They all engaged each other in good-bye hugs then. She held onto Gavin first, then Jasiela. She even hugged Madeline, even though they'd be seeing each other in school.

"Thanks for teaching me how to wear a sari," she said to her.

Madeline laughed. "Anytime," she replied.

"Hey, wasn't *I* the one who helped you?" Jasiela asked, before everyone laughed.

"You're right. By the way, I think we should all thank Jasiela for our bracelets too," Jaiden continued.

They all crowded in and gave her a group hug.

"Oh, and Mishaela," Gavin said. "I should thank you for teaching me to play chess. I'll be sure to show my mum and dad. I'm sure they'll enjoy it."

"They should!" Mishaela nodded. "My parents and my sister and I play together all the time."

"That sounds fun," Gavin agreed. "I'll keep you updated on our progress."

There was a brief silence then.

"Well, then... I guess we should be going now," Gavin hesitantly added.

Jaiden nodded. "Yeah, let's do it."

As if hearing the conversation, the door opened of its own accord. The only thing that was able to be seen on the other side was a bright light.

"So... who's going first?" asked Jasiela.

"Can't we all go at the same time?" Gavin asked.

"It's not wide enough," Madeline pointed out. "Why don't we... go by height, maybe? Or age? Who woke up earliest?"

"Let's just go," Jasiela said, with mock annoyance in her tone. "God. You people are all so indecisive."

They all approached the door; taking a final look at the courtyard, and then, one at a time, all stepping through.

Chapter Fourteen

The Aftermath

After walking through the door, Jaiden's body felt as though it was plummeting through the air. She couldn't see anything at all, because of the complete darkness surrounding her. The only thing she could hear was the rush of the wind flying past her ears. She tried to call out for her friends, but could only barely hear her own voice floating through the atmosphere.

Finally, when she felt as if she had hit the ground, she opened her eyes... and was in her bed; in her bedroom, in her parents' house, in her tiny suburb.

The clock on her nightstand read: 6:15 a.m.

"That felt so weird," she said to herself. "Was all of that... really a dream?"

She sat up, feeling a bit dizzy, and needing to take a moment for her eyes to adjust again. Then her eyes fell to her arms, immediately noticing the two bracelets on her right wrist that she'd made with Jasiela.

Falling back onto her pillow, she smiled.

I guess it wasn't a dream after all.

She sat up again then, and checked her phone, which had miraculously charged. It was Friday.

Well, I have to stay up now; I have to go to school. It looks like only a day has gone by, so I couldn't have missed too much.

She headed for the shower just in case the previous adventure had left sand on her body, then prepared an outfit once she was done; she decided to wear her same pink rebellion dress, with a turquoise lace over-dress instead, and a pair of dark brown boots.

She then went downstairs, where her mother was in the kitchen, probably attempting breakfast early. As she sat the frozen bacon into the sink, she saw her daughter. "You're up early, aren't you?" she asked, smiling. "I guess it'll just be you and me for the next few days, until Dad gets back."

Oh, yeah, that's right; since it's only the next day, Dad is still in Boston.

It felt as if she hadn't gone anywhere at all. Had she been gone for the length of time that had passed here, even though it had only been about three-quarters of a day, her mother would've gone ballistic. She would've called the cops of not only Norridge, but every surrounding city, demanded for her dad to come home that instant, and boy, she'd have gotten a talking-to when she saw her again.

Jaiden smiled to herself then.

If I had to guess why everything seems okay, maybe it's that those rumored goddesses probably found a way for us to cover our tracks. Anything's possible with magic, right? Very cool. But did they have to drop us off here before school? Don't we deserve a day off for our society-saving efforts?

She was a bit disappointed, then, that they hadn't been able to get a more detailed answer on what the whole deal with that village had been. The explanation that Phoenix had given was intriguing, to say the least— and maybe somehow, someday, she'd be able to find out herself what magic was truly capable of.

"So I see you have bacon there," she engaged her mother in conversation.

Her mother smiled, in return. "For breakfast," she told her.

Well, duh.

"Not quite as enticing as the lobster rolls Dad's probably gonna be eating nonstop, but passable," Jaiden replied. "What's the plan, then? Just bacon?"

"I was planning on making us some scrambled eggs to go with it, and maybe some honey-banana pancakes."

Jaiden grimaced then.

I'm trying to be civil with Mom, really. I know she's just trying to be nice. But, ugh! Her honey-banana pancakes are disgusting! She uses chopped bananas instead of a puree, so the texture is all weird, and then she has the nerve to load them up with syrup. One bite of those and you'll be foaming at the mouth like a squirrel with rabies—

Her mother noticed her expression. "Or... we could go get something to eat," she suggested. "I haven't been to that baker over on... what street was that again, Harlem? In a really long time. If I remember correctly, they have some of the best breakfast; especially their pastries."

They do, actually, but right now I'm not in the mood for that either.

"Can you drive me to Mishaela's?" Jaiden asked. "It's about the same amount of travel as the place you're talking about is, anyway."

"I can do that." Her mother looked slightly rejected, but not so much for Jaiden to retract her request.

"Hey, Mom?" Jaiden said then. "Uh... thanks."

"Thank... you?" The statement clearly caught her off guard. "For what this time?"

"For putting up with me, I guess." Jaiden didn't really know why she was thanking her mother, either; just that she felt it was due after everything. After all, she had been very patient with Jaiden, and she knew that things could be a lot worse if her mother hadn't been willing to be so understanding. It was a luxury that not all teenagers got, especially teenagers with Black mothers. "You don't... the way you deal with me shutting you and Dad out could be a lot worse. I'm grateful that you're capable of giving, and are willing to give me space. Even if you don't always, I'm grateful that you do it at all. Not every teenager gets that."

"What... happened for you to be saying all of this, Jaiden? Did you get into something again?"

"Nothing too major." Jaiden shrugged. "Maybe someday we'll be able to easily talk about that type of thing. But right now I just wanna go to Mishaela's, if you have time."

"Well... I guess with the time I save from not making breakfast." She shrugged. "Go grab your jacket."

Jaiden grabbed her jacket, and with little following conversation, her mother drove her to the Pagliardi house. Their house was one of those small beige-colored, ground-level houses, similar to the one the Winchesters lived in. Once they'd arrived, Jaiden hopped out of the car and waved to her mother; and once she had pulled off, turned to knock on the door.

Mishaela was the person who answered. "Hi!" she said happily. "What are you doing here so early? And on a school day?"

"You don't mind, do you?" Jaiden asked her.

She shook her head. "You should know how it is by now. It's pretty much like you're one of us," she said. "Come in. We can eat breakfast together."

The two walked into the house then. Jaiden didn't know what was on for the meal, but it smelled delicious, so she was already looking forward to eating; since the food had yet to be ready, though, the duo retreated to Mishaela's room first, where Jaiden then studied her. Her usually wavy hair was even more so, like if it had gotten wet, and she wore a seafoam green floral-print dress. It was nice to see her in more vibrant colors, in clothes that didn't look as juvenile, but still age-appropriate.

"What?" she asked then, probably noticing that Jaiden had been staring at her.

"Nothing. It's just nice to see you in clothes for people who have two digits in their age, now," Jaiden replied. "The dress really suits you."

"Does it? I was really worried that it didn't." Mishaela smiled. "And it's hard to explain, but I... I think that it's time for me to maybe not play it so safe anymore. With my clothes, but also with anything really. I just finished what was possibly the most exciting and thrilling experience I've ever had in the past fourteen years, and that all started with exiting my comfort zone. There's a lot to be said about it, I'll concede. Plus, I reasoned that, if I was brave enough to do what I did back in that world... I can be brave enough to change up my style every now and then."

"No kidding," Jaiden laughed.

"As a matter of fact, it's almost time for my dad to take me to get a new set of glasses. I usually just get the frames both purple, but I think I might get a pair in one of those wacky patterns. You know, for the spontaneous days. There's this one that looks like a lava lamp that my eyes always gravitate to," Mishaela admitted.

There was a knock on the door then; Chiara, as expected.

"Food is ready," she said timidly. "I can drive you to school after."

"Oh! Thank you, Chiara! Much appreciated," replied Mishaela. "We'll be right down. I have to grab a few things first. Actually, Jaiden, could you head down without me? I just need thirty seconds at most."

"Oh. Uh, yeah. I guess." She shrugged. "After you, Chiara."

As the two were walking, Jaiden said, "Thanks, by the way, Chiara. The whole... pronoun thing. You've been the best at remembering that, since I personally asked Mishaela not to change it."

This clearly caught her by surprise; she had to regroup before speaking. "You don't need to thank me for that. I just hope I was able to help you come to a conclusion about which you prefer."

"Eh. No. Not really, but not your fault, though. Gender is tricky." Jaiden shrugged. "Maybe it'll be clearer to me as I continue to marinate on it, but I appreciate you caring, is what I meant when I thanked you. You've never been obligated to be as nice to me as you are. After all, I'm just your younger sister's friend."

"Maybe I was, in the beginning. But you and Mishaela now share a bond that even rivals the bond I have with her," Chiara replied. "What else can you be, than sis— er, siblings? And if you're siblings, that means you're my family too, and we look out for our family here."

Jaiden smiled. "You've got a point. Now let's go on, I'm starting to starve here."

Everyone ate pancakes and pancetta for breakfast. Conversation at the table was in Italian, so Jaiden didn't really know what was going on, but Mrs. Pagliardi was nice enough, without knowing very much English. That was probably where her daughters had inherited it from. Mishaela always offered to translate the conversations her family had for Jaiden, and she was tempted this time... but still refused. Maybe next time.

"I can drive both of you home too," Chiara volunteered when the three had made it to school. She fiddled with a strand of her long aqua hair as she spoke. "I-if that'll be necessary."

Jaiden was just about to say that wasn't necessary (her mom could do it, or she could walk) when Mishaela said, "Thanks, Chiara, we'll meet you right here."

"Sure. I hope you both have a good day." She walked off, smiling, probably en route to the library or study corridor.

"I'm sure she gets lonely sometimes," Mishaela explained why she'd agreed without asking Jaiden first. "Lack of social ability will do that to a person. It's like giving us a lift makes her feel needed, so I don't have it in me to deny her that."

"Oh," Jaiden said, nodding. "That's believable. Well, Chiara's nice, so I don't mind being around her. Plus, she always has some of the best tunes playing in the car."

"Ah, yes, your anthems of anarchy and liberation," Mishaela said as the duo walked toward the doors of their school. "Anthems that I suppose I have a lot more in common with, now."

"No kidding," Jaiden laughed. "Both of us, really."

"Oh, hey, wait." Mishaela grabbed Jaiden's arm to stop her, before opening her backpack and handing her a piece of paper. "Please don't lose that. I don't have any extras."

"Huh?" Jaiden was confused until she looked down at the paper and saw that it was a very official-looking doctor's note. It was even printed on some fancy paper. She'd completely forgotten about the call she'd made to the attendance office technically being only yesterday.

"You didn't even remember." Mishaela smiled, barely holding in a laugh.

"Yeah, well, at least one of us did, right?" Jaiden securely tucked the paper into her own backpack. "So what's on the agenda today? Library for you again?"

"Actually... I think I'd rather go straight to the cafeteria for breakfast today," replied Mishaela. "I know we just ate, but I wanted to pick up a bottle of apple juice to drink later. And... I was also hoping you were willing to introduce me to that new girl in your art class... if that offer is still available."

"Dude, of course! That's the spirit!" At the moment that she held it out to give Mishaela a high-five, a piece of something fell into Jaiden's hand.

A rose petal... in October?

Jaiden turned, and saw that Mishaela was holding one too. They looked at each other, and immediately realized where it had come from; especially after rubbing the petals between their fingers and being met with a dusting of golden dust.

They exchanged a smile, then.

It really was magic... wasn't it?

So There You Have It (An Epilogue)

That really was a hectic time, looking back on it.

Jaiden was writing in her journal a few months later, recalling the times that she'd spent with her friends in a world they'd never known existed before then.

When I came home after school that day, I found out that Jasiela and Gavin had both friend-requested me on all our socials. I wouldn't dream of doing anything besides accepting. Then, Jasiela gave me her cell number. Since then we've been texting each other a lot, and she's been telling me about her life in huge old New York. For example, she's been working on a lot of clothing designs, and she just became an aunt. She sends pictures, too, mostly of clothes but sometimes of food. You know, the good stuff.

But sometimes, she says, the city just seems too big for her. I wonder if she'd like it here? Norridge is tiny, and there's always the ability to go into the city if small time living gets too boring.

With Gavin, it's a little harder to keep up conversation with him because of the time zone difference, but when I get to talk to him, it's always a fun time. He's really into architecture, so all I have to do is send him pictures of some famous Chicago buildings and he gets all excited over the design and how they must have been conceptualized and all that. We also talk about food a lot too, because London's also a melting pot of cultures, so he's able to sample things from different cultures with as much frequency as I can. We were gonna make it a thing, where each weekend we were gonna pick out a country and go to a local restaurant to try it out, but that first week we chose Indian food and Gavin immediately opted out of the challenge altogether. I thought it was delicious, but I was also concerned at how much he was coughing over video call, so...

Since the whole ordeal, I've started to become closer friends with Madeline, too. Since she's a year ahead of me, I sometimes ask her for help with passing certain classes, and her advice on that is (usually) very, very useful. As long as I stop her before she starts getting too far into her theories, it's a pleasant exchange. Plus, I get to go to her house more often, so I've been seeing more of the twins and their golden retriever. She's started to invite me to her and Mishaela's recitals too. They actually aren't that boring. Who'd have thought I'd actually like classical music? Or at least not hate it.

Speaking of Mishaela, she did get those new glasses, and we sometimes go shopping for new clothes now, as she phases some of her old stuff out. She literally still had clothes in her closet from when we first became friends, that she knew perfectly well she couldn't fit anymore. Oh, and after I introduced her to that cute girl in art class (I found out her name is Lulu), they did end up becoming friends! Honestly, maybe even more than friends, judging by how close they sit together when they eat lunch together— but that's also just how Mishaela is, she also sits really close to me, so that may be just that classic Italian friendliness. I try not to speculate too much; I know that if something serious is going on there, she'll tell me.

In addition to video calling each other sometimes, Mishaela and Gavin actually write each other letters. They take, like, two weeks to get to each other, but the two of them seem okay with that. In his letters, Gavin always makes sure to tell her to "give Jaiden and Madeline a hello," and once he sent me this really interesting book about the architectural history of England that I haven't read just yet, but want to when I have time— It'll give me something to talk to him about, since it merges one of my big interests with one of his. Most of their correspondence is them updating about school and family, though. It is always fascinating to learn what life's like in a whole other country by way of having a friend there.

We're almost sophomores now, and Mishaela's birthday is coming up in June. As far as I know, I've actually managed to pass all my classes, even though I'm pretty sure I just squeaked by in algebra. The Pagliardi girls will be leaving town for around two weeks after school lets out; they go to Italy almost every year to visit family, so it's not a surprise.

She thought, tapping her pencil against her chin, before putting it back to the paper.

I'm not really sure about my summer plans, but I'll probably stay here for the summer, since my dad already went to Boston without me once during the school year. Maybe my siblings will come visit me, if any of them can find the time. Even if they can't for whatever reason, I don't mind.

I've had enough adventure for now.

As Jaiden wrote the last sentence, a distant noise caused her to divert her attention to the window in her bedroom. Closing the journal, she stood up hesitantly before walking to it, cautiously lifting the lower half. With a quick look around, nothing seemed to be amiss, but when she saw a clump of leaves fall off of the tree in front of her house she quickly looked up. Summer was barely approaching; there was no reason for the leaves to be falling yet, was there?

She was immediately stricken with a pointedly negative feeling that was difficult to describe upon seeing one of the tree's boughs. It looked as if it had died; devoid of leaves, purple-tinged, ominous in overall aura. If Jaiden didn't know any better, she'd say it looked a lot like how all the trees of Compositora had looked— the few that had still been standing, at least.

Suddenly feeling a sense of haste she ran downstairs and quickly put on shoes, and continued onto the sidewalk in front of her house. Usually, from here, she could see at least seven trees; what worried her more than the fact that they all seemed to be decaying in the same way as the one outside her window, was the fact that she could only see about five of them immediately.

"But... that doesn't make any sense. Why would our trees disappear, or die in the same way? Our trees aren't made of magic. They're made of... roots and leaves and seeds and stuff."

As she pondered— as her father called for her to come back into the house and not leave the door open like that— Jaiden wondered if that last line in her journal was true anymore.

Had she had enough adventure for now?

Acknowledgments

Thank you to everyone on this page for assisting with the production of this book.

Copy/Developmental Editing: Caroline Macon Fleischer

Cover art: Charity "Ranefea" Santiago

(Special Edition package extras)

Charm design: ArtsyPosey

Stickers and postcard: Michelle Rivera

About The Author

At the age of 8, over a summer with no plans, Michelle decided she would use leftover notebook paper from the past school year and her new lightbox to create a story. This was the activity that occupied her mind for that summer and much of the rest of the year, using the pictures she traced to create a world where the Rugrats and Strawberry Shortcake lived together. This was an activity that she continued to recreate when she decided that first story was done, having been officially bitten by the "writer's bug."

When she entered middle school, notably without any friends to hang out with or talk to on the phone because she was "too weird" or "childish," she then wove a story completely of her own imagination, with original characters: groups of friends being friends, attending class together, going to have lunch together; things she was unable to do in real life due to the lack of friends and strict parents. Her stories took a turn for the mystical and supernatural because of a few factors: the rise in popularity of emo and scene culture, vampire fiction, and her new interest in Japanese video games, particularly role-playing games. Today, she would describe her writing as spiritually similar to such games: the real interconnecting with the magical to create worlds where seemingly ordinary people have the ability to tussle with gods.

Perhaps it is because she wishes to have such power in her own daily life.

Michelle lives in Chicago, IL. While she doesn't have a partner or any children, she aspires to be the keeper of a cat someday. You can follow her on Twitter at @iridescentraynu.